MILLS

THE HEAR

50% OFF
ALL MILLS & BOON
BOOKS IN STORE.

Simply tear off this coupon and
present it with your purchase
from WHSmith.

MILLS & BOON   **WHSmith**

3980 8219

Rachael Stewart adores conjuring up stories, from heartwarmingly romantic to wildly erotic. She's been writing since she could put pen to paper—as the stacks of scrawled-on pages in her loft will attest to. A Welsh lass at heart, she now lives in Yorkshire, with her very own hero and three awesome kids, and if she's not tapping out a story she's wrapped up in one or enjoying the great outdoors. Reach her on Facebook, Twitter (@rach_b52) or at rachaelstewartauthor.com.

MR ONE-NIGHT STAND

RACHAEL STEWART

MILLS & BOON

First Published in Great Britain 2019
by Mills & Boon, an imprint of HarperCollins*Publishers*
1 London Bridge Street, London, SE1 9GF

Mr One-Night Stand © 2019 Rachael Stewart

ISBN: 978-0-263-27129-4

MIX
Paper from
responsible sources
FSC™ C007454

This book is produced from independently certified FSC™ paper
to ensure responsible forest management.
For more information visit www.harpercollins.co.uk/green.

Printed and bound in Great Britain
by CPI Group (UK) Ltd. Croydon, CRO 4YY

My first Mills & Boon has to go to my mum and dad, for instilling in me their passion for books from a very young age.

To my mother, for her wild ways, which certainly shaped my ability to produce work that tends towards the heated end of the spectrum, and to my father, for always believing in me.

My only regret is that my mother didn't live long enough to see me welcomed into the world of Harlequin Mills & Boon—so, Dad, you need to celebrate enough for the two of you now, okay?

Love you both always. Thank you for making me, me.

xxx

CHAPTER ONE

PATIENCE—HE WASN'T known for it. Why should he be when he'd worked his entire life to ensure he got everything he wanted, when he wanted it?

Flicking his wrist, he checked the time. Eight twenty-five.

Where the hell were they?

If being late was a last-ditch attempt at angling for more money, then Tony Andrews was an even bigger fool than Marcus had had him pegged for.

He waved away the approaching waitress who was eyeing his empty glass. He'd already indulged in a whisky and filled his one-drink-while-on-business quota. He wasn't fool enough to indulge in more. Although the girl's perfect parting pout made clear that it wasn't just a drink being offered.

Not tonight. He smiled back.

He might be considered an arrogant ass by many, but no one could accuse him of lacking in manners. Even his questionable childhood hadn't beaten those out of him—much as his father might have tried.

It was hardly her fault he wasn't up for it. She had appeal aplenty, if surgically enhanced assets and peroxide hair were your thing.

But tonight was about work.

And work was work.

Sex was sex.

Never should the two be mixed. Not if you wanted to stay focused and come out on top.

He watched as she weaved her way back through the intimate arrangement of tables, breaking his gaze to scan again the people occupying the circular floor space of the exclusive rooftop venue. Andrews had chosen it for convenience, it being located only two blocks down from his London HQ.

Very convenient for Andrews—*not so sodding convenient for him*. He rolled his shoulders and re-checked his watch.

What the hell was he doing?

He should've left ten minutes after the hour, not sat there like some obedient monkey.

But then, he wasn't there simply to catch up with the man he was in the process of buying out. He was there to be introduced to Andrews' business partner—soon-to-be *his* partner—Jennifer Hayes, before they signed on the dotted line.

Not that the introduction would make any difference; the deal was as good as done. But professional courtesy made him stay. That and the fact he was curious to meet her—the exec who'd turned a business into the largest successful start-up the industry had seen in years.

He was convinced Andrews hadn't been responsible for it. It was a wonder the man could still see straight, with his mounting gambling debts and outside work attentions. And then there was the drink problem. No one had confirmed it, but Marcus was sure he had one. He knew the signs well enough, thanks to dear old Dad.

So, yes, he doubted Andrews had done a full day's work in years—and that meant one thing: Miss Hayes was the one carrying the company; she was the one he was effectively buying into.

He'd read her profile, noticeably devoid of any pictures, and figured her to be late thirties, early forties. A woman with shrewd business acumen, a bearing that bordered on cold, and a definite force in the boardroom—all of which he'd respect her for. So long as they were on the same page.

It intrigued him that he hadn't come across any pictures. Not even a professionally enhanced shot used to support all those public accolades. Maybe she didn't go in for that kind of vanity. Or maybe Andrews did all that for her. He was certainly everywhere. Even the *Forbes* article he'd thrust into his hands at a charity auction last month, when he'd put forward his proposition, had highlighted the success of the business but featured Andrews alone, his greased back hair and cocky grin filling half the page.

The memory of that expression goaded Marcus further now as he waited and waited, fingers drumming on the tabletop, his patience hitting breaking point.

Seriously—enough was enough. The papers would be taken care of in less than twenty-four hours regardless. He might as well meet her then.

Tugging at the cuffs of his shirt, he made to stand up just as the cables of the glass elevator started to shift. *New arrivals?*

He settled back and waited for them to come into view.

It wasn't Andrews. That was immediately obvious. The small, balding lift attendant was being dwarfed by a statuesque redhead who made even the impressive lift look small. He wasn't the only one noticing either. Her hair was pulling every eye in the room. Its cascading waves ran down her back, glinting in the ambient light, impossible to ignore.

Its dramatic colour was a striking contrast to the black dress that clung to her curves before halting modestly at the knee. His gaze dropped lower still, to her exposed calves, to the subtle shimmer that teased with the possibility of stockings. And then came her shoes, her severe black stilettos…

Heat assaulted his groin.

Fuck me.

He wasn't going anywhere. Not just yet. Andrews could have the extra time for free…

Jennifer glanced at her watch and cursed under her breath. Eight-thirty. She was late. She hated being late.

But then, what did Tony expect, calling her at the eleventh hour and asking that she meet him for drinks? The blasted guy should know better than most what kind of workload she had.

Hell, who was she kidding? He couldn't give a shit what her to-do list looked like. Truth was, *he* was the cause of most of it. His increasing absence these last couple of weeks was pushing her to the brink and sending her stress levels through the roof. And yet here it came, that little voice in her head…

He has so much going on...he needs you...his family needs you...

But, hell, *her* family needed her too—her mother and her sister. Not just financially, but physically, and he was stretching her so thin.

But you owe him. He doesn't owe you. There's the difference.

She let go of a slow breath, easing the tension out with it, and gave the lift attendant a polite smile of gratitude. He returned it to her chest and she sighed anew. *Seriously?*

Stepping past him, she adjusted the deep V in her wrap-around dress and cast her eyes over the softly lit room. *Where are you, Tony?*

His gregarious personality was enough to project a homing beacon, and the room was decidedly absent of it. Most people were split into couples or foursomes—all save for one man. Her breath caught, a peculiar awareness taking hold.

He sat at a table beside the glass wall. A great seat from which to enjoy the far-reaching cityscape below, although his eyes showed no interest in the vista. No, they were well and truly pinned on *her*, projecting an intensity that had her skin prickling with such thrill.

Hell, she wanted to stride straight over—the urge was almost making her do just that—but sense prevailed. Tony wanted to see her. Hopefully he could explain away his crazy behaviour, and put her mind at rest over the future.

Giving a small sigh, she headed for the bar. A drink—that was what she needed. Anything to take the edge off.

Slipping onto a bar stool, she crossed her legs and replaced her clutch with the leather-clad drinks menu.

'Good evening, Miss Hayes, what can I get you?'

She looked up to find Darren, the head bartender, approaching with a smile, his hands busy drying off a glass. She returned his smile easily and scanned the list, honing in on a vodka martini and figuring that had to be strong enough.

He cocked an eyebrow when she made her request. 'Shaken, not stirred, *madame*?'

His Scottish-accented Bond impression had her laughing, and the sound was alien to her ears. It had to be weeks—months, even—since she'd had a proper giggle. Maybe *she* was the one in need of a good shake, never mind the drink.

'However you recommend it.'

'You sure?' He raised both brows. 'It's pretty strong.'

He knew her too well. She didn't do spirits. A spritzer was her usual drink of choice. But a spritzer just wasn't going to cut it. Not tonight. It wasn't just Tony, it was her increasing concern over her mother too. She was getting worse and there was nothing Jennifer could do to stop it.

Her heart fluttered painfully and she pushed the thought aside. *Not now.*

'Sounds perfect,' she said, flipping open her clutch and retrieving her mobile to check if Tony had at least messaged. But she'd not even lit the screen before her eyes sidled away, drawn to the brooding silhouette not twelve feet away.

He was tall—she could tell that even with his body folded into the deep bucket seat. The ankle of one leg casually rested atop the knee of the other. The designer cut of his dark suit and tan leather shoes spoke of money, although whether he had any was an entirely different matter. She'd learned that quickly enough in the city. People only had to dress to impress and it attracted wealth like bees to honey.

But there was something in the broad set of his shoulders, accentuated as they were by his tailored jacket, and the confident air in his relaxed poise that had her certain he wasn't all about the front.

And what a front...

Her eyes drifted upwards. The crisp white shirt sat smoothly over his torso, no hint of spread. Then they drifted higher, to the last fastened button of his open collar and the hint of dark hair curling there.

Her pulse skipped, her mouth watered and her eyes snapped back to her phone. *Not now!*

Seriously, what was *wrong* with her? Was she that desperate to get laid? That fed up with her trusty vibrator that her body was putting up a fight? Truth was, there was no time in her life for that complication. Mr Dildo didn't talk back, didn't require care and affection. He didn't require time that she didn't have.

Between her office and dashing back and forth between London and Yorkshire each weekend to be with her family she was all out of that.

But one night, though. Think of the possibilities...

Heat simmered low in her belly as she activated her phone screen. *No notifications.* She fired off a brief Where are you? message and placed the device back on the bar, her heightened awareness picking up on movement from the man's direction. She watched him crook his finger to the blonde waitress hovering nearby and an inexplicable pull ripped through her.

Christ, he was reeling her in too.

She nibbled the inside of her lip, drinking in his rakishly long dark hair, the chiselled set to his jaw that softened delectably with his easy grin. And then there were his eyes—so compelling. She couldn't make out the colour, but there was something about them, something deliciously sinful…

Her tummy contracted with a barrage of heat, and in that second she knew she wanted to leave with him. That she wanted one night of crazy. No names, no real talk, just wild, no-holds-barred sex.

Could she do it? Hell, would he?

It wasn't in her nature, it wasn't like her, but being 'like her' was hard fucking work and she needed this…needed him.

Mentally, she undressed him, button by button, stroke by stroke, her thighs clenching tight in their folded position.

'One vodka martini.'

'Huh?' Her eyes snapped to the bar, to Darren placing a mat and glass before her.

'Your drink.' He smiled teasingly. 'Distracted, much?'

'Quite.' *And that was an understatement.*

Warmth fed her cheeks as she took hold of the olive stick propped inside her glass and began to stir with it, her focus on the mini-whirlpool she created while she set her thoughts to chill.

Get the meeting with Tony out of the way first.

Raising her drink, she sampled it, a small hum of appreciation escaping her as the chilly temperature contrasted with the burn of alcohol in a strangely pleasing way. She took another sip and felt her shoulders start to ease, her posture soften.

Ah, Tony, maybe you've done me a favour, dragging me out.

She rolled her head on her shoulders, her eyes seeking him once more— *Fuck*. Their gazes collided, the invitation in his sending lust tearing through her.

To hell with Tony, and to hell with doing what was right all the time!

Just give him twenty minutes...

Gah—She forced her attention to her phone and issued him a text that said as much.

Five minutes later, fizzing over with the prolonged wait, she caved and beckoned Darren over.

There was no harm in putting things in motion.

'You're not ready for another?'

She grinned, high on the thrill. 'Please...'

He chuckled. 'Okay.'

Placing a fancy tray of bar snacks in front of her, he set about making her drink.

She eyed the food, her tummy growling. She'd missed dinner again. Taking up a few snacks, she savoured one before asking, 'Do you know what Mr Distraction is drinking?'

He sent her a knowing look. 'You wanting to send him one?'

'Maybe...' Playfully, she popped in another snack, chewing over it and relishing the instant hit of salt. 'So, come on—do you know?'

He smiled as he worked, his eyes flicking briefly to the man in question. 'He's a J&B man.'

She licked her lips clean, her eyes flitting to Smoking Hot Guy, and then to his bottle of choice on the shelf. Hot Wealthy Guy… J&B… An image of the hottie in *American Psycho* flashed before her eyes and she swallowed, hard.

Okay, Okay…yes, you want a night of crazy, but maybe you should know something about him first.

'What's got you looking so serious?' Darren asked, picking up on her shift in mood.

'I was just wondering…' Her voice trailed off as she considered the talented bartender. Darren knew everyone that came and went. 'What do you know of him?'

'Can't tell you much.' He strained the liquid into a fresh glass. 'I've not seen him before, but there were some guys at the bar talking about him earlier. Recognised him from some article or other.'

Her ears pricked up. 'An article?'

'Yeah, you know the sort—one of those professional mags, I reckon.' He popped an olive in the glass and placed it before her. 'He's a CEO in the technology field.'

She sucked on the inside of her lip, suppressing the surge of excitement. *No CEO was going to turn out to be a nutcase.*

'Well, fancy that…'

'You sure do.'

She grinned and plucked the olive from the glass, popping it between her lips as her eyes hit Smoking Hot Guy's.

Damn sure I do!

CHAPTER TWO

IF HE HAD to watch her pop another olive in her mouth, her eyes alive with wicked suggestion… He circled the rim of his glass with his index finger, the move rhythmically in line with the heat coiling through him.

He really should've left when he'd got the bail-out text from Andrews. Instead he'd sent a brief acknowledgement wrapped up in a warning.

Be at the solicitor's nine a.m. prompt for contract exchange or else.

And then he'd settled back.

He really should've been more annoyed too, but it was fascinating what the sight of a blazing-eyed redhead enjoying her fill at the bar could do. And he wasn't just referring to the olives—there were the bar snacks too. Whatever they were, they had her licking her lips and her fingers with such teasing that between that and the olive-sucking his lower body couldn't get a let-up.

And, Christ, those eyes—they pierced him from across the room. The warm lighting of the bar glinted off their depraved depths as they came back to him again and again, demanding his attention, drawing him in, giving him hope that she wasn't waiting for someone else to appear.

She was chatting to the barman now, her perfectly poised body leaning in as they exchanged words, their easy flow of conversation suggesting she was probably a regular. The guy nodded to her and moved away, freeing her once more, and he sensed her attention returning to him. His breath halting, his hand paused over his glass. And then her mobile lit up and her eyes dropped to it. She gave a flicker of annoyance and then a smile. She tapped at it and placed it back on the bar.

Now her eyes came to him and, *fuck*, were they calling.

His gut clenched, his jaw tightened and the room disappeared. *Something had changed.*

'For you, sir.'

Not now. Grudgingly, he looked to the voice and found the blonde waitress hovering, a tray with a lone drink resting upon her palm.

'J&B.' She took hold of the glass and bent to place it on the table. 'From the lady at the bar.'

His gaze dropped to the glass and he smiled.

Hell, Andrews, you've actually done me a favour.

From her elevated vantage point upon the bar stool she watched him straighten and plant his feet, the move sending her heart into her throat.

Oh, yes, come for me...

He lifted his glass off the table and started towards her, his tall, imposing frame filling her vision, his eyes lighting up every nerve-ending in their path as they raked appreciatively over her.

She turned on her stool to face him, sipping at her drink as she waited until he was within earshot, and then she smiled. 'It's lovely of you to join me.'

He tilted his glass. 'I wanted to thank you for the drink.'

Wow, that voice. She drew a breath as her body flared. It was deep, husky, rough...the perfect mix for a body that exuded power. And that accent—she couldn't place it, but it was there, teasing her.

'And I wanted to thank *you* for improving my outlook this evening.'

He rewarded her with that easy grin, his eyes sparking and pulling her in. They were the colour of chocolate, the dark and rich kind, and they were on fire, burning into her as he said, 'You and me both.'

'Is that so?'

'You *know* so.'

'I know no such thing.'

He gave a small chuckle and reached past her, placing his glass on the bar. She twisted into his arm on impulse, felt his scent invading her, the heady masculine cologne sending lust slamming into her core.

'Perhaps I can convince you over another drink?' He leant back against the bar-edge. 'What can I get you?'

What could he get her?

She wanted to laugh as the word *you* rode on the tip of her tongue but instead she looked to Darren, 'I'm already being taken care of.'

He followed her gaze. 'Is that another vodka martini?'

'It is.' She smiled, her fingers toying with the empty stick still floating in her glass. 'I think I've found a new favourite drink.'

His eyes travelled from her to the stick. 'It's quickly becoming one of mine too.'

She could take a guess at why. She would have said as much if he hadn't spoken first.

'So, what brings you here?' He angled himself to-wards her, his forearm resting on the bar-top, his fingers coming to hover just above her knee. 'Beautiful woman, no companion—it just doesn't fit.'

Beautiful? She loved how that sounded coming from him, loved how close his fingertips were reaching. If she just uncrossed her legs they would brush against her, those long, capable fingers that were sure to possess such skill...

'Business or pleasure?' he probed.

Her eyes shot back to his, her thighs clenching anew. The way he said it—*pleasure*—it rolled off his tongue like a physical caress.

'I was meeting someone...' She was barely aware of the words coming out of her mouth.

'Was?'

'They cancelled.' She lifted her empty stick and nibbled at its end, needing to do something—anything to keep herself busy. 'What about you?'

He eyed the stick, a pulse working steadily in his jaw as he took up his drink once more. 'Business.'

She could hear it then, in that one simple word, an edge to his voice. A barely contained need that matched her own.

Her attack on the stick ceased, and her breath was

shallow as she struggled to say, 'Are you finished for the evening?'

'Never even started,' he said, that same husky edge to his voice teasing beneath her panties. 'Lucky for me, they cancelled too.'

'Lucky?'

He nodded, his lips quirking over his drink as he took a sip.

'And why's that?' she said, dropping the stick to caress away the strain building in her throat.

'Isn't it obvious?'

'Maybe—but I'd like to hear you say it.'

He placed his drink on the bar, his eyes coming back to her, ever closer. 'Do you always get your way?'

'Most of the time.'

'Why is it I can believe that?'

He reached up to brush her hair behind her ear, his delicate touch sending an excited ripple through her, and then he trailed it down, the ripples multiplying exponentially.

'What makes you say that?' she asked, barely audible.

He studied her, his eyes dropping to her lips, their depths flashing darkly as she swept her tongue out to ease their sudden dryness.

'I get the impression you can be quite persuasive.'

She knew what she wanted to say, knew it was brash, knew it was out of character, but... 'Does that mean I can persuade you into an evening of pleasure?'

His brow flickered, the only show of surprise at her proposition, and then he grinned: a slow, heart-stopping smile that unveiled a dimple in his right

cheek, the boyish feature at odds with the virile mas-
culinity emanating from the rest of him.

'Is that what you're offering me?'

'Would you accept if it was?'

He leant closer still, his breath teasing at the delicate channel of her ear. 'Why don't you try me?'

Heat flooded her breasts, her belly, her blood, and
the world around her evaporated as she twisted into
him, her lips instinctively seeking his...

'Your drink.'

What?

Her disorientated gaze swept to the bar, to Darren
sliding her drink before her.

Oh, God!

'Thank you,' she blurted, hurrying to mask the
swamping disappointment. But he spotted it anyway,
his smile apologetic as he picked up her empty glass
and moved away.

'How about we take this conversation to my table?'
came the appealing proposition from alongside her.

She brushed her fingertips across her lips, now
thrumming with their near encounter, and flicked
her eyes back to his. 'I'd love to.'

He'd had to work hard to stop himself from saying
place instead of *table*. And still he wondered—would
she have said *I'd love to* in that soft, balmy tone if
he had?

She gazed up at him with those green come-to-bed
eyes and he wished he'd found out.

'After you,' he said, gesturing to her.

He made to pick up their drinks and then stilled,

his concentration broken by the sight of her slipping from the stool.

Between the uncrossing of those seriously long legs and the cleavage he was working hard not to drown in he found himself rooted. Her height impressed him once again as she met his eyeline, her scent wafting up to him.

Not that he had any idea what herb or flower was involved in the making of it. But he liked it. *A lot.*

'Don't forget the drinks,' she threw over her shoulder with a provocative smile, her eyes sparkling with mischief, desire, amusement… He hadn't a clue.

It was taking his all to keep the conversation flowing and his own desire in check. Trying to read every fleeting expression that crossed her face and not jump to the conclusion that she was on the same desire-driven wave as he was nigh on impossible.

Grabbing the drinks, he followed her to the table, his eyes fixed on the sway of her hips, the fall of her hair as it brushed along the gentle flare of her bum.

What it would be like to have that same hair flung across his bedspread? Or wrapped around his fist as he drove himself into her—? *Fuck, he was getting hard just thinking about it.*

And there she went again, staring up at him as if he was seconds away from being devoured.

Now, perched on the end of the low-slung seat that had remained vacant at his table, her head came cock-high and heat rushed to his groin in greeting.

Adding to his pain, she crossed her legs, the action forcing her dress to ride high and reveal the top of a stocking, he was sure, before she righted it.

Too late. The damage was done. And she knew it.

She'd watched the entire thing play out in his face. And, hell, he wasn't even convinced the low lighting was enough to conceal the bulge down there.

He held out her drink. 'For you.'

'Thank you,' she said, her delicate feline fingers slipping over his own to take it from him.

The contact was soft and brief, but total dynamite to his over-active imagination as the image of her taking hold of something else ransacked his mind.

He watched as she lifted the glass to her glossy full mouth and tilted it, the clear liquid flowing into her as the olive bobbed at the base of the drink. And then she closed her lips and swallowed, her tongue emerging subtly to take away the remnants. The sight was sweet perfection to behold, utter torture to his straining cock.

'Are you going to sit?' she said up to him, her raised expression making it clear she had caught him staring, good and proper.

Did he care?

Did he fuck!

'Apologies,' he said, dipping his head in mock regret, his grin telling her he wasn't sorry at all. 'I confess to getting lost in the sight of you.'

It was corny, it was overly smooth, but again he didn't care. It was the truth.

He placed his drink on the table and took his own seat, feeling her eyes upon him the whole time. The nature of her thoughts penetrated the air.

'A penny for them?'

Her smile widened. 'Something tells me a man like you should know well enough that you never ask a woman that question.'

He gave an easy laugh, staving off the heat raging below his waist. 'What if I said there's something about you that makes me want to ask that question regardless?'

She set her glass down and pressed her elbow into the arm of her chair, leaning in towards him.

'Then I would tell you…' she began, her voice low and husky, each word spun out as her fingers took up a slow caress over the exposed valley of her chest. 'In that case I would divulge *exactly* what I'm thinking.'

He would have—could have—dragged her away from the bar that very second. The way her eyes beckoned him, the way her wandering hands lured him, the blood surging to his cock—it was all getting too much and he hadn't so much as touched her.

And, fuck, did he want to.

The need ravaged him. He wanted to taste every last bit of her, stroke her until she begged for him to complete her, fill her body until she could do nothing but scream his name.

And yet she couldn't. They had shared a lot in a few electrifying glances, but they hadn't so much as covered the basics of *My name is…*

They should at least get that covered. 'Perhaps we should start with introductions?'

She laughed. 'Introductions?'

'Yes,' he said, surprised at her reaction. 'You know—me Tarzan, you Jane, before we get carried away with this—' he waved a hand between them '—undercurrent.'

'Undercurrent?' she repeated, her eyes dancing over the word, her fingers still doing their crazy damn tour of her body. 'You know, I think you've summed it up perfectly.'

His eyes followed her fingers, his control teetering as he succumbed to the pull of her caress.

'So?' he pressed, his brain only half on the attempted introduction.

'So…?' she mimicked teasingly, the action both maddening and arousing. And then she dropped her hand to take hold of the stick floating in her drink and all thought of conversation disintegrated, obliterated by the sight of the inoffensive little green ball slowly being stirred around.

It was coming—he knew it—and the power of that sight, up close and with every alluring detail to feast upon, had his knuckles turning white.

'Who needs names in this day and age?' She lifted the olive out of her drink and tapped the stick against the rim of the glass to rid it of excess vodka. 'Don't you think there's something to be said for leaving a little mystery?'

She looked at him on the last word, the stick pausing to rest against the glass edge. 'It's not like I'm here looking for a meaningful relationship.'

He wanted to say something smooth, but she had him stoked to silence. The perfect package was at his disposal—sexy sophistication brandishing a *fuck-and-leave* policy. He didn't do relationships—they were for the weak and the needy. And, hell, if you weren't weak at the off, you soon would be when it fell apart or, in the case of his dad, got ripped away. Then it would ruin you.

He lifted his glass and took a careful sip, swallowing down the unwelcome memories and throwing his focus onto the attractive bundle before him. 'You and me both.'

'Well, then, wouldn't you rather…' she leaned across the table and brought the olive to her lower lip, her cleavage forming an alluring backdrop '…we just got the hell out of here and had some fun?'

She parted her luscious pink mouth and popped the olive inside, her lips closing around the stick as her eyes held his with deliberate tease. Then slowly, painfully slowly, she pulled it out, her lips rolling outwards as they held the olive inside, stripping the stick bare.

'I make that three olives now.' His voice rasped, his mouth drying up at the inviting slickness of her lips.

She considered him, her throat moving captivatingly as she devoured the green ball. 'Three—really?' She smiled playfully, dropping the stick into her glass with a ting. 'You're very observant.'

'When something's worth observing I'd say I am.'

'Is that what I am? Worth observing?'

'You with that drink—*definitely*.' His voice was tight with the effort of holding back, and his lack of control was so alien he knew he was in trouble. But right now he didn't care. 'In fact, if I was a religious man, I'd say the devil invented drinks such as those.'

'The devil?' Her brow furrowed and she nibbled thoughtfully at her lip, the innocent gesture smashing the last of his restraint. 'Because of the corrupting alco—?'

'No,' he interjected, pushing himself out of his seat and striding to stand before her.

She looked up at him questioningly, her throat bobbing as she swallowed. He knew he'd surprised her but, he couldn't wait any longer. To hell with where they were.

Reaching for her hand, he took hold of it and tugged her to her feet, the force sending her unresisting body right up against his own, her eyes flashing as they lighted on his mouth so close to her own.

'Because they make me forget all decency and do this…' He cupped her chin and roughly took her mouth in his, his tongue taking no prisoners in its desperation to sink inside.

An explosion of sensations went off at once. She tasted like heaven, like the olive, the vodka, the traces of gloss across her lips… And then she sighed, the soft, feminine sound escaping her lips as she gave way to his invasion and he lost himself in her. Her hands snaked through his hair, her tongue seeking out his own, twisting and flicking, tasting and probing…

His surroundings disappeared as every sense focused on her: her kiss, her smell, the feel of her breasts pushed up against him, the little sounds she was making, the desperate buck of his cock as it pressed into her lower belly.

There was a movement behind him, the brush of a chair and a muttered 'Excuse me.' It filtered through his brain, through the haze.

'Get a room,' a voice said.

His internal voice or a real person? He didn't know. He didn't care.

But he should care…

He should!

Reality came crashing down—he needed them out of there. *Now.*

Forcing himself to slow down, he tried to part their

mouths, their faces. He was rewarded with her teeth nipping at his bottom lip. A playful protest that felt anything but…

'Spoilsport,' she complained, and her pout was to die for.

He took a steadying breath. 'You're cheeky, sweetheart.'

One hand still cupping her face, he freed his other hand to rub it across his own, trying to get himself composed. He should be more unnerved by his lack of self-control—but fuck did he want to run with it regardless. Something told him that letting go would be worth it. That *she* would be worth it.

He scanned the bar. No one seemed to be looking their way. But that wasn't to say they hadn't been seconds before. That voice had sounded real enough.

'We were having fun,' she said, drawing him back, her eyes wide and alluring.

'We *were* having fun.' He repeated her words. 'But I think we could have more fun elsewhere. I can have my driver here in five?'

Her eyes flittered and his chest tightened. *Was she going to refuse him?*

'Driver, you say?'

'Yes.' He moulded his free hand into her back, pressing her against him, against the hard swell of his cock. *Don't deny me.* 'I promise he will see you home safely…after…'

He continued to caress her lip with the pad of his thumb, loving how her tongue would dart out sporadically to moisten the path for his touch.

'In that case you'd best call him,' she said softly, her hand coming up to take hold of his fingers and pressing a chaste kiss to their tips. 'I'll go and settle up.'

And just like that she was on it, stepping out of his hold and taking up her bag from the table, heading for the bar. He watched her go, his eyes hooked on the sweet sway of her body, he blindly retrieved his phone from his jacket pocket. He dropped his gaze just long enough to dial his driver and, efficient as ever, he answered in two rings.

'I need you outside in five,' he said into the phone.

'Sure thing, Mr Wright. Where we heading?'

'Home.'

He cut the call and thrust his hand through his hair. He didn't take women home. He went to a hotel, or their place. That way he could leave when he was good and ready. Certainly before morning. But the thought of sharing this woman with an audience a second more, or navigating the whole reservation thing…. He didn't have the patience. Or the inclination.

But to take her home—what the hell was he playing at?

CHAPTER THREE

JENNIFER TOOK HER time heading to the bar, sensing his heated gaze upon her and wanting to give him a worthy show. Her posture was smooth and assured, her hips moving with teasing provocation, her hair swinging subtly with each step.

On the outside she screamed control, but on the inside... She was on fire for him. The blood pumping through her system was heated beyond comprehension.

She wanted them alone. *Now*. But racing to the bar was hardly going to scream sex appeal and the very idea brought a laugh to her lips.

'Good night?' Darren said, not missing her little eruption.

'The best,' she said, placing her clutch on the bar and sliding onto a stool.

'Glad to hear it.' He gave her a knowing grin but left it there, his professionalism overriding as he asked, 'So what can I get you?'

'Both bills, please.'

'Sure.' He raised a cocktail shaker to the side of his head and started rattling it with gusto. 'Give me one min.'

'No problem.'

She propped her elbows on the bar, her head resting on her hands as she watched him work. She likened herself to the contents of the metal contraption being so expertly worked in his hands—shaken and about to be devoured. She smiled blissfully, the idea suiting her just fine.

It amused her that he'd wanted her name. It was a sweet gesture—*too sweet*. She didn't want sweet. Sweet only led to complications—the kind that brought feelings, even relationships. And there was no place in her life for any of that. Her career came first. Her career and her family. She had no time for more. Not yet.

No matter how hot, how sexy, how interesting...

She twirled her hair around one finger. No, she needed him to be all about the sex—definitely just the sex. Someone like him would be too dangerous, too much of a distraction, to have around for long.

But as for the here and now... A little shiver ran through her as she conjured up those eyes, that smile, the dimple.

She glanced over her shoulder. He was on his phone but he was watching her, just as she'd known he would be, the carnal blaze of his eyes heating her from across the room.

'Here you go.'

Darren's voice pulled her back to the bar and his outstretched hand, containing a silver tray with two bills. She slipped her card on top, trusting him implicitly to have it right. 'Just pop it on there.'

'No problem.'

His eyes flicked behind her as he moved to the till

and she realised her impromptu date had moved. She could sense his approach radiating down her back, her fine hairs prickling in anticipation beneath the delicate fabric of her dress, and she strung the sensation out, waiting for Darren to return her card and wish her goodnight before she turned.

'I hope you don't mind…' she said, looking up, and her words went the way of her brain, combusting on the pull of his eyes, that smile, that dimple…

He raised a bemused brow. 'Mind…?'

She smiled through the desire. 'I settled your tab too.'

He looked surprised. 'You did?'

'I did.' His reaction amused her. 'Do you always look this surprised when a woman pays her own way?'

'I can't say I'm used to it.'

She rolled her eyes. 'Well, welcome to the modern world.'

He laughed, the sound husky and amplifying her already spiking libido.

'Point made,' he said, placing his hand in the small of her back and stirring up a truckload of nerves. 'Shall we go?'

She grinned up at him. 'Unless you want this modern woman to throw you over her shoulder and carry you out, I suggest we do just that.'

His laugh deepened and the desire to kiss him, to feel that excited resonance against her mouth had her on fire.

Soon, Jennifer!

She forced her legs to work and they headed to the lift, noticing that this time the attendant chose to avoid looking at her all together. What a nice change.

Even nicer still, the hand on her back started to wander, his fingers moving to caress rather than hold, his heat penetrating the thin veil of her dress and making her tremble.

He bent his head, his mouth hovering close to her ear, 'Are you cold?'

She fixed her gaze straight ahead, fear that she would set upon him and give the attendant an eyeful making the glass doors suddenly riveting. 'No.'

But two can play at that game, she told herself, sidestepping in front of him, just enough so that she could conceal her hand as it made contact with the front of his thigh.

He gave a sharp intake of breath, his thigh tensing beneath her splayed fingers and making her smile in satisfaction. *Payback!*

He was a delight to explore. The strong rigidity of muscle flexed as she stroked upwards, circling from his outer thigh to the inner—

His hand shot to her arm, his fingers gently gripping her in what she assumed to be a silent message to behave.

No chance.

As the lift descended she teased and coaxed until his hold eased enough for her to reach her target—his very tip. Lightly she brushed up and over. He hissed against her ear and her belly coiled with exquisite heat.

She traced around him, revelling in his growing reaction, coveting his size, his girth, his length...

She filled her hand and squeezed. He bucked within her palm, a cough erupting from his throat, and her smile grew as the lift came to a gentle stop.

Before them the doors opened, and she released him with a playful tap, stepping forward to exit with the attendant. He followed close behind.

The private hallway was deserted. Sounds of the busy city reached them from outside, but the window-less entranceway blocked it all from view.

'Have a good evening,' the attendant said, stepping back inside the lift and pressing the button.

She watched the doors close and the lift start its ascent, waiting for the attendant's eyes to be out of sight so she could

Whoa!

Startled, she found herself being spun into him, her eyes and mind barely registering his hold before he was propelling her back against the cold marble wall, his lips coming down to crush her own. He pinned one hand to the wall above her head; his other running up and down her side in brutal exploration.

Heat exploded within her, the ache between her legs flaring with such force she wanted to cry out as she kissed him back, her hands thrusting through his hair, her tongue delving into him, fighting with his own as she desperately sought more.

But he tore his mouth away, pressing his forehead against hers, his ragged breaths sweeping down her front. '*You* are a tease.'

'You started it.'

She yanked him back to her. He obeyed for a split second, his tongue flicking teasingly into her mouth, and then he was breaking away to travel down her neck, his teeth nipping and grazing with dizzying effect.

'*God, yes!*' she cried, head arching back, hands invading his jacket as she strove to feel every bit of him. The hard muscles of his chest twitched and flexed as she explored—smoothing, clawing, pulling at his shirt.

The hand at her side reached the hem of her dress and he shoved it upwards, his fingers gripping the underside of her thigh as he lifted it, forcing her to wrap her leg around him.

He raised his head to gaze down at her, his hand tracing the band of her stocking, tension working in his jaw. 'You're dangerous.'

'You like?' she said, trying to focus through the haze.

'Love.'

He twanged the suspender and she gave a heated shrug, shoving a hand through his hair. 'It's a power thing.'

He growled, the sound animalistic, lighter fuel to her raging heat as his mouth reclaimed hers and both hands took hold of her thighs to lift her entirely against him. The cool air swept over her damp panties, followed sharply by his rock-hard cock, its trouser-clad presence driving against her. She bucked with delight, her mouth breaking free to let go a frenzied moan.

'I'm losing my mind,' he said into her collarbone, feasting on her skin as he thrust her upwards, bringing the valley of her chest to his face, his hot breath and slick tongue creating an insane combination that had her breasts pleading for him.

But suddenly he froze.

'Shit.'

She looked down at him, her body writhing, her

lungs struggling for air. And then she felt it—the phone in his jacket vibrating into her thigh.

'It'll be my driver,' he said, his voice gravel-like and rumbling through her.

'Of course,' she breathed, fighting for control over the insane rush and thriving off it all the same.

Shaky, she lowered her legs and he helped her, waiting until she was safely on her feet before shrugging his jacket into place and fishing out his mobile.

He stepped back, tapping at the screen and raising it to his ear, his other hand trying to put some order back into his hair. The sight made her smile. *She'd* done that to him. He'd let her. They'd both lost all control and the realisation was exhilarating.

She worked to straighten out her clothing, her hair, her racing body. All the while telling herself she should be grateful for the interruption, that indecent exposure wouldn't go down well for either of them.

But the thrill of it. Of him. In public—here and now... It appealed *too much*.

'On our way.' He spoke into his phone and then cut it off, slipping it back into his pocket and turning that sexy, *fuck-me-now* smile on her as he offered his arm. 'You good to go?'

She nodded and hooked her arm in his. 'Let's be quick about it.'

He gave a laugh and together they strode down the hallway and out of the building.

Directly outside, on the congested street, squeezed into a parking space she could scarcely believe it fitted into, sat a pristine black limo, its driver waiting at its rear. He straightened as he set eyes on them, and she knew for certain that this was the driver he had spoken to.

If any doubt had remained over what Darren had told her then it would've been wiped out now. Yes, he was definitely CEO material. A very successful CEO at that. She was considered successful herself, but even she didn't possess the wealth that brought with it this kind of service. Or maybe she did...she just didn't get to see any of it...

'Evening, Mr Wright,' the driver said as they approached, his eyes dropping briefly to her as he gave a respectful dip of his head.

Wright?

She smiled up at him. The name fitted him well—he certainly felt like *her* Mr Right.

But then he could be called Mr Tickle and she'd probably think it just fine right about now.

'Colin,' her Mr Wright said, 'this is Miss...' He faltered and looked down at her.

She realised he was at a loss, thanks to her enforced air of mystery, and gave a laugh. It all seemed rather ridiculous now. As if they needed any mystery to add to the fire already searing between them!

'Miss Hayes,' she said, beaming at his driver. 'But, honestly, you can just call me Jennifer.'

His arm froze in hers and his eyes narrowed, a look she couldn't identify sweeping across his face. Something about it panicked her. But then it was gone, his eyes were calming, and he looked back to his driver.

Had she imagined it?

It was dark...the street lighting wasn't great...

'This is Miss Hayes,' he said.

Hadn't she just told him that?

'And she needs a lift home.'

What the fuck?

'Home?' She couldn't keep the surprise out of her voice.

Just then the heavens opened—great big dollops of water raining down on them just as she would have said more. They hunched forward against the onslaught as the driver swung open the rear door and told them to get in. He would get the address from them when they were safely inside.

Pulling her with him, he forced her to fold into the back seat of the car. Her brain was rambling, trying to come up with a reason—any reason that didn't imply an end to the evening's affairs.

He wouldn't have the audacity to lead her on and then... No, it wasn't possible. He must be suggesting they both go to her place. But that wasn't happening. That was *her* domain.

She waited for him to close the door before she sidled up to him, her fingers toying with the top button of his shirt as she hooked her head beneath his chin.

'It's a nice idea to go to mine, but if it's all the same I'd much rather go to yours.'

He didn't say anything and she gazed up at him. He was staring at a point over her head, and the taut lines of his face sent the hairs prickling at the back of her neck.

'Is something wrong?'

His eyes flicked to her and away again. 'I'm not sure this is a good idea.'

'You can't be serious,' she said, her hand stilling, her eyes falling to his mouth and the grim line now forming there.

She hadn't imagined his need. It had mirrored her own. If he was having a last-minute change of heart out of respect for her feelings, and all that sentimental crap, then she would see to it that he forgot it.

She let her hand trace down his front and felt his body turn rigid.

Outside, traffic sped past, delaying the driver's attempt to round the vehicle and get inside. She had time…

Lifting her head, she used her nose to brush the hair from behind his ear. The scent of his dampened hair product was fresh and masculine, tantalising her as she pressed a kiss to his skin, her tongue flicking out to taste. His jaw clenched and his arm at her back tightened, neither gripping her to him nor moving away.

'I want you,' she whispered into his ear, and his breath hitched.

His waning resolve urged her on. She nuzzled him as her hand slid down his front, over his torso, the buckle of his belt, his zipper, to his left thigh, where she knew the length of his cock lay. She felt it swell obediently into her palm as a curse ripped from his throat.

Victorious, she used her teeth on his lobe. 'See… you want this too.'

She gripped him hard and he inhaled sharply, a hiss forming through his teeth.

She traced the edge of his ear with her tongue as her hand started to move over him, around him. 'Just tell me you don't and I'll stop.'

'Jennifer…' He groaned her name as he pressed

back into his seat, his lower body riding upwards to increase the pressure of her hand.

'That's it, baby,' she cooed. 'Feels good, doesn't it?'

'Fuck, yeah,' he rasped, and she felt her carnal prowess take a bow, the power going straight to her head, liquid heat pooling between her legs.

The front door yanked open—*shit!*

They both sat bolt upright, like a pair of teenagers caught in the act, faces flushed, eyes wide.

The driver clambered in and glanced over his shoulder, his expression one of pure professionalism, as though they hadn't a hair out of place...or several—

'Where to, sir?'

'Home.'

The driver's brows lifted. '*Your* home, sir?'

'That's what I said.'

Then he hit a button that had the privacy glass sliding up.

Was that stuff really private?

She was about to ask when he took hold of her hips and swung her over his lap, the speed of the move sending a surprised gasp from her lips that swiftly turned to a moan as she found herself over the very hardness of him, her knees straddling him, her dress thrust up to her hips. He raked a hand through her hair and yanked her mouth down to his own, his tongue pillaging, his hands rough upon her thigh and her hair.

Hooking her hands around his neck, she clung to him, desperate to keep their mouths connected while her body started to ride his clothed hardness in mindless abandon.

Vaguely she was aware of his hands shifting, his

fingers hooking beneath the dress at her shoulders and shoving it down, imprisoning her arms to her sides.

He broke away, forcing her back so that he could look at her.

Her breasts bloomed under his burning gaze, her nipples straining beneath the light padding of her bra. He brought his hands up to shoulders, his touch now gentle and prolonged as he slid them beneath the straps, taking them down to meet the ruched fabric of her dress before returning to smooth over her shoulders and down her front.

She bit back a whimper of anticipation as he met with her bra and then he slipped his hands inside, his heated palms brushing fleetingly against her taut and swollen peaks before they dipped to cup her, the brief contact an erotic torture as they begged for more.

'So beautiful...' he said softly, his hands weighing her in his palms as his thumbs stroked upwards, their pads meeting with her pleading buds and rolling over them.

Pleasure shot through her, and she threw her head back as a moan tore from her throat.

'You like that?'

'Yes!' she cried. The heavenly combination of his hands on her body and his hardness at her clit had her rocking wildly, and she could feel the tell-tale tension mounting.

'I need to see you.'

With those gruff words he took hold of the band of her bra and tugged hard, forcing her breasts to spill out. He groaned, his head coming forward as he closed his mouth around one stiff peak, sucking it back into the cavern of his mouth, teasing it and then releasing it to let his teeth nip, his tongue lap. He did the same with the other, one hand coming up to join in the attention, his fingers pinching and rolling, his palm groping.

Outside, a car horn sounded as another torrential wave of rain pounded at the roof. The worldly sounds were a reminder of where they were, but it only served to take her higher, every bit of her becoming a tense powerhouse about to crack.

'I'm gonna come...' she moaned. 'I can't take... I can't...'

His answer was to nip harder, to drive her hips against him, to encourage her further, higher than she could ever remember being with any man. And then she was crying out. Her body was going into spasm as wave after wave consumed her. She heard him groan as he buried his head in her chest, holding her against him, taking each rock of her body until she was spent.

With cheeks flushed, she made herself straighten, conscious of time passing. 'How long do we have?'

'About twenty minutes.'

He traced a hand down her back and she shuddered at his lustful gaze. 'Perfect.'

'Is that so...?'

She made an affirmative noise as she bowed to press a kiss to the bridge of his nose, his lips, across his jawbone... Reaching his neck, she flicked her tongue out and revelled in the salty essence of him, knowing he was overheating at her hands.

'And why would that be?'

His voice cracked on the last word as she cupped him, her fingers testing the rigid length of him. She was desperate to expose him to her hands, her gaze, her mouth…

'It's time enough for me to return the favour,' she said, placing her hands on his thighs and slipping from his lap, coming to nestle on her knees between his feet on the floor.

The car took a bend and she steadied herself using his legs, her fingers biting into his flesh.

'Easy,' he said, taking hold of her arm and using his free hand to gain purchase on the trim of the car.

She smiled up at him. *Christ, he was so hot.*

She wanted to imprint the sight of him in her mind, all dishevelled and feverish. The feeling of excitement at having him at her mercy, the heat of his grip on her bare arm, the cool air of the car keeping her exposed nipples pert and alert. Her clit had barely recovered and the throb was back with a vengeance.

She dropped her eyes to his belt, to his zipper, the fastening taut as his hardness pressed against it. Her mouth salivated as she smoothed her hands along his thighs until they reached the object of her fascination.

'You are truly beautiful,' he said, the hand at her arm dropping to cup her breast, his fingers and thumb caressing her sensitised skin.

The knowledge that he was enjoying the sight of her semi-nakedness was just as thrilling as his touch. She bit her lip against the resurging tension. *It was his turn.*

Forcing herself to concentrate, she fed the leather of his belt through the loops. The metal from its buckle jangled as she parted it, the sound oddly thrilling, making her fingers quiver as she undid his button. Then, taking hold of his zip tab, she paused to look at him from beneath her lashes.

'You can tell me to stop, if you want?'

She was purposely teasing him, needing to have the memory of his earlier hesitation forgotten, obliterated by his total surrender.

And she had it.

He looked to her with almost pained ferocity, his expression dark and erotically charged as he thrust one hand into her hair. *'Fuck, no.'*

She gave him a wicked grin, his impassioned response going to her head as she slid the zipper down. 'That's better.'

CHAPTER FOUR

BETTER—IT WAS fucking better.

But then…

It could hardly get any worse.

Marcus threw his head back, his hands flying to the edge of his seat, eyes squeezing shut as he tried to push out the moral judgement threatening.

He shouldn't be letting her do this. They shouldn't be doing this. *When she realises who I am…when we have to work tog—*

Her fingers slipped around his cock, killing off all thought as his eyes shot back to her.

Fuck, she was beautiful!

Her green eyes, vibrant and captivating as they flicked between his own eyes and his crotch, seared him, blinding him to the reality of the situation and the gravity of it.

She pulled him out and gave a small gasp, her eyes widening as she took in his entirety. Her open appreciation was like rocket fuel to his swelling erection. Then she moved her hand over him, her gaze wrapped up in the sight of him, and the heat surged forcibly to the head of his dick, his thighs trembling beneath him. He gripped the side of the car tight, his teeth gritted tighter.

He was going to shoot his load over her any moment.

'Jennifer...' The effort of forming her name made him sound pained.

But she didn't even break focus. Her hold tightened and her dainty pink tongue flicked out to moisten her lips. The move was so carnal and electrifying he bucked within her fingers and she shot him a look, cheeks flushed, eyes hungry.

A groan tore through his throat. Beautiful didn't even cut it!

She was still half naked, her arms restricted by her dress, her tits propped upon it and pressed together while she explored him, their darkened peaks luring him, the valley between tight and evocative. How he'd love to thrust himself inside that channel, watch as he jacked all over...

Fuck! She's going to be your business partner! She has no idea who you are!

Salacious heat spread through him. He was damned. No matter that he knew it was wrong. The idea had now brought an erotic twist which swamped all else and had pre-cum escaping his swollen head. He looked down to catch her brushing across it with her thumb, its pad spreading it teasingly down the underside of his cock, her eyes marvelling like he was the best thing she'd ever seen. And then she met his eye, bowed her head.

Fuck, fuck, fuck!

His nails bit into the car's upholstery, his eyes fixed on hers, pre-cum seeping anew, and blindly she dipped to taste him, flicking out her delicate tongue and cleaning him like a fucking ice lolly.

His glutes clenched. 'Jennifer…' he breathed.

He was so close.

She answered his plea with a smile that screamed smut and slid her mouth over him, surrounding him with her inviting wetness. The head of his cock collided with the back of her throat, blood rushing to feed it, and his mind turned dizzy with the heat streaking through his body.

She undulated, circling her tongue the length of him as she sucked him back, her free hand slipping down between her legs to work herself at the same time.

Fuck yeah!

The sight had his cock ramming into the back of her throat and she gagged, the sound obliterating all remnants of his control.

Releasing his hold on the car seat, he shoved his fingers through her hair. 'Take it!'

She moaned in response, the sound guttural, vibrating around his plundering cock. He heard her take a breath through her nose and then she sank, burying him in deep. He'd never felt anything so intense, seen anything so goddamn erotic. This redhead, on her knees, with his hands rammed in her hair, her cheeks hollowed out as she worked the whole of him throat-deep, her hungry eyes glittering as she watched him, her arm shifting frantically as she got herself off.

He pulled her head up, the suction making his balls contract, and her eyes looked to him in lustful surrender, telling him to dictate, to drive…

'Fuck, sweetheart.' He drove her down over him, setting her to his rhythm, his depth.

The cabin was filled with the smacking sound of her cheeks. In and out. In and out.

He wrapped her hair around his fist, his other hand gripping at the seat-edge as he lost total sight of where they were, who they were. All he could see now were those lustful green eyes and that perfect mouth, his cock slick with her saliva…

He wanted to warn her, but his orgasm ripped through him, its force blowing his mind as he held her head still, watching himself explode into her, her eyes sparking as she drank him in.

She took his all like a heavenly drink, her mouth moving over him as her moans filled the cabin, her body rocking between his legs as her own orgasm claimed her.

He didn't want to blink, didn't want to miss a second. He softened his hold in her hair, his fingers starting to caress rather than hold, his eyes absorbing the vision that she was.

When she eventually shifted to straighten her clothing he helped her. She smiled at him, her hands slipping her breasts back into her bra.

The brief sight was enough to make him wish he could go again. And he would go again—no doubt about it. Very soon.

He knew that tomorrow would bring with it a hell of its own, but for tonight their fates were sealed, and he wasn't letting her go until he had her in his bed and was buried inside her.

'Thank you,' she said, wiping her fingers across her swollen lips.

Now, *that* made him laugh. She had him doing that a lot. 'I think I should be thanking you.'

'My two to your one—I owe you,' she said matter-of-factly, pulling her dress into place and climbing back into the seat.

'You *owe* me?' *Hell, he liked the sound of that.* 'In that case, thank away. I'll be calling it in shortly.'

'Thank you,' she said again, softly, her eyes dancing as she leant in and pressed a brief kiss to his lips.

His mind exploded with the image of her naked and sprawled across his bed. He was supposed to be righting his own clothing, and yet the desire to pin her back in his car burned through him.

Christ, none of this boded well for the future.

He zipped up his trousers in self-disdain. He didn't do sexual distraction. Not on this level. And definitely not at work. But that was exactly what the future held.

He was going to have to function alongside her for however long it took until he was sure the business was working towards the strategy he wanted. Until *she* was working towards the vision he depicted. It might be a fifty-fifty business partnership, but experience dictated that things went a whole lot more smoothly the quicker people came around to his line of thinking.

Would she be any different?

Fuck knew.

Especially now that he had screwed her. Had let his dick get in the way of all good sense. All good business sense.

Ah, hell, get over it!

They'd had sex—simple as. He hadn't known

who she was at the outset. He'd tried to stop it. She'd pushed.

She'd wanted nothing serious. And he had delivered.

It would be fine.

His gut twisted. It wasn't fine. He'd let his libido get in the way of business. *Hell, he was still doing it.* He *never* let that happen. The moment he'd known he should have shut it down. *Hell, he should be shutting it down now.* And yet...

Alongside him she wriggled in, and instinctively he wrapped his arm around her, pulling her up close. *What the hell was he doing?*

She gave a tired sigh. 'This feels nice.'

Nice? Jesus, his lips actually twitched with a smile. She thought this was *nice*?

He shifted back in his seat, testing his head against the curve of plush leather and finding it surprisingly inviting. *Okay, so he could see the appeal...*

Had he really never done this before? Lain back in his chauffeur-driven car and relaxed. He scanned the roof of the vehicle, the soft fabric and the lights designed to soothe, and realised the answer was a definite no.

He shouldn't really be doing it now either. Not when he could be catching up on emails, phone calls, the latest press releases in the technology field, or pondering the potential shit storm about to hit between himself and his new business partner...

She gave a small sound, the comforting noise at odds with his inner wrangling, and he quit, pushing everything away but the feel of her body curling into his own.

He would deal with it all when the time came, but for now…

'Sir, sir… Mr Wright!'

The noise was incessant, as was the shaking pressure on his shoulder. *What the fuck?*

His head shot up, his eyes flying open in disbelief. *He'd fallen asleep!*

He pushed through the brain fog, registering the heavy warmth of his companion on one side and the chill attacking the other through the open car door. He looked to the hand on his shoulder and then to its owner, leaning in from outside—Colin.

The driver met his gaze and promptly straightened, his hand falling away. 'Sorry, sir.' He cleared his throat. 'When you didn't respond on the intercom I gave you an extra twenty minutes. When I tapped on the glass and you still didn't respond…' He gave an awkward shrug.

'It's okay, Colin.' Marcus spoke softly. He wasn't ready to disturb her. She was so peaceful, curled up almost childlike against him, her breathing deep and even. She was out of it.

How tired can she be?

A foreign emotion curled around his gut, the force of which had his eyes snapping away. He was being a fool—they couldn't very well stay there.

He looked to his driver. 'I'll rouse Miss Hayes and then you can get off for the evening.'

'It's fine, sir. I'll wait and take her home when you're ready.'

'No,' he said on impulse. 'She can stay with me for the night.'

If Colin was surprised he knew better than to say anything. Hell, Marcus was surprised enough for the two of them. None of this was *normal*.

But then, *she* was far from normal. She was *the* Jennifer Hayes. His head spun anew. How could he have pegged her so wrong? He'd deemed her older, colder, nothing like the intoxicating bundle now hauled up against him.

She had achieved so much, and yet there was no way she was even his side of thirty. He tightened his arm around her, admiration going to his head even while anxiety crept in.

No, he definitely couldn't let her go without explaining who he was, what he would be to her from nine a.m. tomorrow, clearing the air and dealing with the fallout.

Goddamn you, Andrews!

If he'd only turned up and done what he was supposed to then none of this would have… *Ah, hell!* He didn't want that either. He wouldn't wish away their evening—not if his life depended on it.

But there was no denying it was a bloody mess.

Next to him, Jennifer stirred.

'Hey…' He bowed his head to hers. 'We're here.'

She mumbled and snuggled down further, teasing out a smile from him despite his creeping unease. A gust of cold air swept through the car and she wrapped her arms tighter around her chest but made no attempt to rouse herself.

He looked to Colin. 'Get the doorman to escort us. I'm going to carry her up.'

'Of course, sir.'

He disappeared off and Marcus turned his attention back to Jennifer. Settling her down on the back seat, he slid out of the car and reached back inside, his arms hooking under her. She folded into him naturally, her head dropping into the crook of his shoulder, and he was straightening up by the time Colin returned with the doorman.

'Bring her bag, please,' he said to him, and then to Colin, 'I'll see you at eight.'

Keen to get her out of the cold, Marcus headed into the building. The doorman, complete with bag, beat him to the waiting elevator and swiped the card for the penthouse.

As they ascended Jennifer rubbed her face against him, her delighted little noises doing weird things to his chest. He knew the doorman was doing his damnedest to stay professional, working hard to conceal his bemusement at the situation. Marcus couldn't blame him. It was weird for him too.

What the hell was he doing?

He should have woken her up, got her address and had Colin take her home. But even as he acknowledged the thought, he dismissed it. This way he had a chance to keep control of the situation, tell her who he was and get it dealt with.

The lift came to a stop, the doors opening onto his private foyer, and he stepped out. He gave directions for the doorman to leave the bag and bade him goodnight. Now he was standing in his vast suite, his creature comforts surrounding him, and there was a woman he barely knew curled up in his arms.

For the first time in his adult life he had no idea what to do and, boy, did it grate on him.

If she'd been awake it would have been different. There were plenty of options that sprang to mind. Like an honest conversation, for one. As well as the not so virtuous options which, despite his recent release, still got too much of his vote.

And for that reason alone he didn't dare wake her. Not yet.

He needed his control firmly in place before she set those evocative eyes on him again. Bizarre, really, as his control was the one thing he had always been able to depend upon. But it had fallen by the wayside tonight.

It had to be the illicitness of it all. Surely once the cat was out of the bag it would all become entirely manageable. *She* would be manageable.

He looked to the various doors. There were two bedrooms. He could put her in the guest room. It was nice, cosy enough. His body immediately rejected the idea, and his mind came quickly to its aid—*You can't leave her to wake up without you. She'll have no idea where she is.*

It was a good enough reason for him.

Striding purposefully towards the master suite, he told himself he was doing right by her and kicked open the door. Reaching his bed, he pulled the covers back one-handed and set her down.

She turned into the mattress on contact, her body relaxing as he pulled the quilt to her chin, her long, lithe form folding into the charcoal-grey as if she belonged.

A warmth spread through him, irking him to turn away and head for the door.

Since when did the sight of a woman in his bed appeal?

The truth was *never*.

Because he'd never let it happen before.

Behind him, she gave a soft moan, the sound lulling his resistant gaze back. She shifted, her hands hooking into the pillow beneath her head and drawing it closer. His throat closed, his body heated, and he had to force his legs to work, to stride from the room straight down through the foyer and into the living area, where his glass drinks cabinet beckoned.

He debated how much he'd consumed already. Not quite two J&Bs. He could stand another. Just one.

Pouring himself a careful measure, he went to take it up when his phone buzzed with the arrival of a text message.

He pulled it out and checked the screen, his hand clenching around it as his stomach turned over.

I've been calling you for a week. Since no police have rung I assume you are still alive and just being ignorant. Call me back. Gran x

A bittersweet smile pulled at his mouth—*she was never one to mince her words*—and guilt swamped his unease. Yes, he should have rung, but no matter how he played it, how he tried to talk himself out of it, his grandparents, for all their devotion, brought with them the past.

And the past could go fuck itself.

Still, he owed them a call.

Hell, he owed them many.

Fingers moving deftly over the screen, he promised them he'd be in touch and then placed it on the side. Taking up his glass instead, he glanced down into the swirling amber liquid and felt his stomach turn anew.

Fuck.

He swiftly put it down, the harsh twang of glass hitting glass barely registering as the memories flooded him, his hands falling into fists at his side as he tried to push them out. The painful reminders of where pain and booze could take someone, of the many beatings he'd endured with the stench of drink permeating the air, of his father, so broken and twisted—

Let it go. You're not him. You never will be.

He strode to the glass wall, his sights fixed on the glittering city lights, and took a breath, trying to empty his mind and finding it impossible.

And then he thought of her—the distracting bundle curled up in his bed—and, no matter the trouble that was coming, he felt something inside him ease.

CHAPTER FIVE

IT WAS THE scent that hit her first—the hint of male cologne, all warm and woody and decidedly comforting to Jennifer's sleep-addled brain. She wrinkled her nose into the plushness cushioning her head, revelling in its luxurious feel. So soft. So nice. Much nicer than the feeling coming off the rest of her.

She stretched out and froze. She was still fully clothed. The jagged edges of her underwear bit into her skin; the brush of the quilt against her stockinged legs and the pinch of her stilettos was alarmingly peculiar.

And then came a faint noise, the unmistakable sound of snoring.

Jennifer slept alone. *Always* alone.

And now she was awake, cocooned in the scent of male and definitely not alone!

She shot up, her hands fisting into the sheets around her, her eyes blinking rapidly as she adjusted to the darkness of the room. It was huge. The bed she was in was huge, the floor-to-ceiling glass walls taking up half of the room were huge.

And then she saw him—her Mr Wright—his sleep-slackened body reclining in an armchair at the opposite side of the room, his silhouette outlined by a view of the moonlit Thames.

This had to be a dream.

But if it was a dream surely she would remember going home? Surely her every sense wouldn't be on high alert?

Then it all came flooding back. The bar, the elevator, the car ride to his place. Everything. In all its flaming hot glory. And in spite of her clothed discomfort she felt her body heat; her breasts flushed and her clit came alive.

He was exquisite. Even in the dusky light she could sense his power, feel his appeal...

His jacket lay across the arm of the chair, his forearm resting upon it. His other arm was folded, his hand curving over his inner thigh, his trouser-clad legs relaxed and spread. Open and vulnerable. The sight did things to her, things with a potency that almost scared her, and she flexed her fists into the bunched-up fabric of the sheets.

How could one man have this much effect? She should have been sated and at ease now. Ready to throw her all back into normality and sneak away. No need for goodbyes. They'd both got what they wanted. But...

Her eyes travelled up the length of him, pausing over the open collar of his shirt where the top four buttons lay undone. Her throat dried at the exposed hint of chest, the arousing arch to his neck as he fell back against the curve of the chair, his chest falling rhythmically with his gentle snores.

Fascinated, she folded back the bed covers and planted her feet to the floor, inwardly wincing as her imprisoned toes made painful contact with the ground.

She dipped to remove one shoe and then the other, her toes curling blissfully into the plush fabric of the bedside rug as she smiled.

Had he thought it too intimate to remove them while she slept? Did he not care that her heels had likely damaged his expensive bed linen?

Pushing off the bed, she padded towards him, not really knowing what she was about and half expecting him to awake at any second and pin her with that desire-provoking gaze.

But he didn't move. His breathing remained heavy and even, each raspy intonation teasing at her senses.

As she came to a halt above him her gaze fell to the side table. His mobile, an unfinished glass of what looked to be whisky and her clutch resided there. She glanced at her watch—it was three-thirty in the morning. It was time she left. But even as she thought it her body balked. The idea of leaving without enjoying him one last time, of resisting the desire already burning, was too much.

Beads of perspiration pricked between her breasts and across the back of her neck. Her skin was clammy and her dress made her feel claustrophobic from sleeping in it. The need to be out of it had her hands taking up the hem and pulling it over her head.

The cool air swept across her skin, over her exposed nape as her hair was lifted away, and a delightful shiver ran down her spine.

She couldn't leave.

Not yet...

Letting the dress slip from her fingers, she stepped

forward, her knees coming up against the chair-edge between his legs. She leaned forward, placing one hand on the chair-arm while the other brushed away the hair that had fallen across his forehead, her eyes scanning his beautiful face.

Stunning even when in slumber, this man could ruin all her best laid plans if she gave him the chance, she was sure of it.

But a last goodbye… *Where was the harm?*

Lowering her mouth to his, she brushed her lips against him, tasting the whisky on his breath and repeating the move. His lips gave way beneath her coaxing pressure and she dipped her tongue inside. He was yummy—all warm, whiskyed up and tantalising to her senses.

His eyes fluttered, his hand twitched and then his eyes opened, wide and surprised. 'Jennifer?'

'Shh…' she said, pressing her index finger to his mouth and loving the heated firmness beneath her touch. She dropped her head to flick her tongue out, let it probe alongside her finger, tasting him, teasing him.

He tried to move beneath her, his hands coming up to take hold of her waist, his touch searing through her skin, but she wasn't ready for him to take control.

'Stay,' she commanded, raising her head to gaze down at him, her hands pressing into his shoulders as she pinned him back in the chair.

He looked up at her, his eyes dark and glittering in the low light, his entire body rigid as he succumbed to her will, freed her so she could focus on the fastened buttons of his shirt. One by one she undid them, all the while her eyes fixed on his.

And he watched her, his gaze burning into her eyes, her lips, the valley of her chest, then moving down to the V of her legs as she stood before him, his hands shifting to caress the lace band of her stockings with mesmerising intent.

She tugged the shirt out of his trousers, releasing the last of his buttons and parting the fabric for her hungry eyes. Her mouth like sandpaper, she took in each exposed inch, stroking the shirt off his shoulders, feeling the heat of his skin burning through her fingertips, his muscles rippling beneath her caress. The only sound in the room was their elevated breathing, and her ears were attuned to every hitch in his as she traced her fingers over him, toying with the smattering of hair across his pecs, her thumbs circling each puckered nipple before travelling lower.

He sucked in a breath, his anticipation clear, and she smiled, her fingers closing over his trouser fastening. No belt this time. One less hurdle. Popping the button free, she worked the zip, her hands brushing his hardness with their movement and sending her clit on a frenzied dance.

Pinning one hand on his hot, naked shoulder, she slipped her other inside his briefs, felt her own breath catching as he bucked into her palm. He was so big, so hard and ready.

She flicked her tongue out to moisten her lips, a whimper leaving her throat as she looked at where she held him, drawing him out, her hand sliding over him.

'*Fuck!*' He gripped her thighs, fingers biting. '*I want you.*'

Her eyes met with his own. 'I want you too.'

Straightening, she reached for her clutch as the

hands over her thighs slid inwards, his fingers seeking her out. She flicked open her bag.

He slipped beneath her thong, one finger gently brushing against the swollen nub of nerve-endings and sending her bucking against him. He did it again and she moaned, her head gliding back, her attention on the bag momentarily forgotten. He rolled her clit, working her to fever-pitch with his perfect rhythm, perfect pressure, perfect everything.

She rocked against him, biting into her lower lip as she tried to stave off the spread of tension long enough to locate the little foil packet tucked inside her bag.

Pulling it out, she tossed the clutch to the floor and used her teeth to break it open. He groaned beneath her, the fingers of his free hand coming up to probe at her opening, teasing, plundering, teasing some more.

She was on the verge, her mind screaming *Not yet* as she forced herself to step back, to break his touch.

He slumped in the chair and she dropped to her knees, reaching out to take hold of his rigid length and offer him up to her mouth. She flicked her tongue across his tip and he hissed, his hands flying to her hair, his eyes burning down into her as she smiled her pleasure.

Bringing the condom to his head, she held his eyes and rolled it down, securing it to his base before standing and closing the distance once more.

'Take off your bra,' he commanded suddenly.

She bit into her lip again, the tightness in his voice making her body overheat as she dutifully did as he asked, undoing the clasp and letting it fall away.

He cursed under his breath, his eyes burning into her chest as her breasts fell free, their sensual weight goading her clit, their tightened nipples singing in the exposure.

'Turn around.'

Again, she did as he asked. She could feel her wetness slick between her thighs as she moved, the skimpiness of her thong offering no protection from her readiness for him.

'I want you to sit on me,' he said, his hands coming up to take hold of her hips.

An erotic shudder broke through her and slowly she lowered herself, one hand slipping her thong to the side, the other coming down to take hold of his length and position him at her entrance.

His very tip teased its way in. A delicious heat engulfed her and she sank herself down, crying out and clenching him tight as he filled her so completely, so perfectly.

He gave way to a ragged breath. *'Fuck me, baby...'*

His reaction went straight to her head, to her clit, to her core, and then his grip on her hips squeezed as he lifted her up and over him, again and again. Slow at first. Savouring. And then more rapid, more desperate.

His chest came up to press against her back, his hands thrusting up to her breasts, his palms groping, his fingers toying, their attentions ferocious with his own need and driving her own.

'You're so fucking hot.'

She moaned her response, her hands biting into his thighs as she propelled herself over him.

'Here.' He took hold of her hand, brought it to her breast and squeezed her palm over her own flesh, showing her what he wanted. *'Christ, yes!'*

Her other hand flew up, mimicking the mindless caress at her other breast, freeing his hands to take control of her hips once more, giving her the rhythm she craved.

'Yes, yes, yes…' she cried, her head rolling back as she gave herself up to the tension spreading through her like wildfire.

He caught at her thong, pulling it taut over her clit, and the pleasure-pain was intoxicating as he continued to thrust her over him, pushing her to the brink.

And then she exploded, the sensation shattering through her, her muscles clenching wildly around his cock and taking him with her. The tremors of his body mixed with her own as he encased her in his arms and gripped her to him, taking them both back against the chair.

He rested his chin on her shoulder, his uneven breaths tickling at her flushed skin. It was blissful and bittersweet. For a goodbye, it had to go down as the best she'd ever had.

'We should talk,' he said suddenly, his chin jutting into her flesh as he spoke.

His words had the effect of an ice shower on her overheated body but she didn't tense up, didn't want him to sense her unease.

'Later—or rather, in the morning,' she said calmly, turning her head into his and pressing a kiss to his temple. 'First you need to get some proper sleep. What possessed you to take the chair?'

He shrugged, his grin warming her anew. 'What can I say? I'm nothing if not a gentleman.'

'You call what we've shared this evening gentlemanly?'

'Point taken, yet again,' he said, manoeuvring her so that she sat across his lap, his sated cock slipping out to rest beneath her behind. 'Not complaining, are you?'

She gave a laugh. 'What would you do if I was?'

'You don't want to know.'

It was how he said it, rather than what he said, that had her body heating with mutinous anticipation. She wanted to press, wanted to coax the words out of him but didn't dare. He played to her carnal desires so effortlessly, so perfectly...

'Is that so?' she said simply, it was a question, but it didn't ask for a response, and to ensure he got the message she snuggled down into his shoulder, her mouth clamped shut as her disgruntled body tried to force out a moan, her mind conjuring up a variety of reactions to her potential complaint.

'Not tonight, though, hey?' he said, pressing a kiss to her head and standing effortlessly with her in his arms.

He strode to the bed, his legs taking a wide stance as he kept his trousers in place. In spite of her emotional turmoil she laughed, his gallant candour leaving her momentarily on cloud nine. And then he deposited her on the bed, breaking their contact.

'I'll be right back,' he said, straightening and heading for a doorway that she assumed led to the bathroom.

'Don't be long,' she called after him, turning into the quilt and preparing her *I'm fast asleep* pose.

She didn't want to risk delaying her departure with conversation. She just needed to leave—and she would once he was asleep. A sudden heaviness hit her, deep in the belly, and she wrapped her arms tight around her middle, fending it off.

She'd had her one night of crazy; she'd had her fun. It was time to get back to reality—a reality without Mr Distraction in it. It was for the best.

It really was.

CHAPTER SIX

SHIT. SHIT. SHIT.

The words had been echoing through his brain for the last two hours, ever since he'd woken to find her gone. The only evidence she'd ever existed was a hurried *Thank you x* on a scrap of paper placed on the pillow.

Thank you. He had been worth that, at least.

But gratitude was the last thing she'd be feeling shortly. In just over an hour, when he turned up at her office and told her who he was, he was certain he could say farewell to a thank-you or a repeat.

A repeat.

He wanted to shake himself. *Was he mad?*

Sex was sex. He could get it anywhere.

What he couldn't get was another business partner like Jennifer Hayes.

He could hear his body laughing at the idea even as he shot the thought down.

Work had to come first. He would tire of her eventually, as he had every other woman. She wouldn't be any different—he wouldn't allow it.

And he wasn't about to put it to the test.

He needed to get the situation under control, and

swiftly. He just had to hope he hadn't screwed their working relationship along with her.

But she was a professional and he was banking on that to save him from too much of a scene in the office. It wasn't the ideal location for delivering the news, but what choice did he have? A phone call wouldn't cut it—not when she could simply hang up. And he wasn't about to risk her getting wind via anyone else.

He was also banking on her sound business acumen making her realise that ultimately his presence in the company could only be a good thing.

Plus, they'd both had fun. That had to count for something—*right?*

He combed his hand through his hair and wiggled the knot of his tie. Stress really wasn't in his make-up…

Across the table Tony Andrews sat in discussion with his solicitor. Documents were being passed to and fro, and the scratch of pen on paper broke the air as each one was signed. But the buzz that usually accompanied such a sound was non-existent, drowned out by the very real possibility that he was heading into World War III.

His own solicitor, to his right, leaned towards him. 'It's not too late, you know…'

It wasn't the first time he'd said that this morning. He was astute. He knew Marcus. Had worked with him for a decade. He knew something wasn't right and assumed it was the deal.

'No, it's all good, Roger,' he said, his gaze resting on Andrews as the man looked to him questioningly. He saw the flash of relief in his eyes before he looked back to the paperwork and wondered yet again at the man's situation.

He was clean-shaven, smartly turned out, his blond hair greased back as per usual, but it was his eyes and the dark circles beneath that told of the stresses beneath the slick exterior.

There was also a tell-tale scent that one might mistake for an overly strong cologne if one wasn't as attuned to it as Marcus. It didn't matter that he'd spent two decades free of it, of *him*, it still affected him as if it was yesterday. As if he was still that little boy hiding away as his father rolled in night after night, intent on taking out his demons on the one person unable to evade him.

His nails bit painfully into his palms and slowly he unfurled his fists, forcing himself to relax, throwing his focus into Tony Andrews instead.

He would feel sorry for the man if not for the fact that he'd brought it on himself. Or the fact that Jennifer was suffering as a direct result. She was clearly hitting the point of exhaustion if her tiredness last night had been any indication. If Andrews had been a decent business partner who pulled his weight she wouldn't have been in such bad shape.

Jennifer... He gritted his teeth. He never should have believed her when she'd suggested they talk in the morning. He should have known it was bull.

Christ, how many times had he done that himself? Escaping before morning, before all the questions and the hopes for a future...

His ego took the hit even as he respected her for the move.

And what did it matter? Soon she wouldn't be able

to walk away from him. He felt the buzz then—the spark of excitement in his gut.

'Mr Wright, if you could do the honours?'

Andrews' solicitor beckoned him, twisting the pages of the contract so they were facing his way and sliding them across the polished wooden surface of the table.

'Of course,' he said, taking up his pen and signing as Roger directed.

With each scrawl of his name the passion thrived, the excitement, the buzz... Only it definitely wasn't this acquisition that was doing it. It was *her*—Jennifer—being tied to working under the same roof as him.

The confusing realisation should have bothered him—*but did it?*

He couldn't see past the buzz to care.

Jennifer was having the morning from hell.

Tony letting her down last night was one thing. Tony not turning up to the morning's company-wide briefing was something else altogether. How could the employees trust their direction if he hadn't even turned up to deliver his part?

She gave way to a groan and collapsed back into her chair.

'Hey, don't stress—you did a great job.'

She looked to Anna, her optimistic, ever-cheery personal assistant, and smiled. 'I could've walked in there wearing a pink tutu, reading a fairy tale, and you would still tell me I'd done a great job.'

Anna set a fresh coffee down on her desk, her face lighting up. 'Ooh, now there's a thought—one for the next briefing, hey?'

In spite of herself, Jennifer laughed and took up the drink. 'I'll make a note.'

'Great,' she said. 'And while you're doing that I'll go and see if I can track down our elusive Mr Andrews.'

'Thanks, Anna.'

Anna turned on her heel and headed for the door, pausing on the threshold just long enough to say, 'You know, maybe you should take a leaf out of his book some time and take a break. Leave him to pick up the pieces for a change.'

Jennifer gave a non-committal snort. Anna meant well, but seriously, there was no way in hell she would leave the company in *his* hands. Not now.

She looked out to the buzzing office on the other side of the glass wall, to the employees she had a duty to protect, and decided she had to push for his signature on the Shareholders' Agreement. She didn't like to force it, but it was time.

Her solicitor would certainly be relieved. He'd made no bones about how stupid he thought she'd been to continue operating without one. But, hell, she'd been naïve and young, thinking some great gift had come her way when Tony had offered up the joint venture. She hadn't thought for a second that he would change so much, that he would destroy her trust so spectacularly.

Her mind decided, she wiggled her mouse to wake up her computer screen and Marcus Wright stared right back at her, filling it up.

Yes, she'd looked him up. Yes, it had been the first thing she'd done when she'd hit the office at seven a.m.

It hadn't taken her long to find out enough. It was

surprising she hadn't come across him, considering they worked in the same industry. But then she didn't focus on the people, rather on the companies and what they were churning out. And she knew of his company plenty well enough.

As for him—he was big news. Well-regarded, highly esteemed—not only in the business world but for his charity work too. His name came with accolade after accolade. The perfect chocolate box mix. And now she'd sampled him how was she supposed to move on?

She groaned again. Her head landed on her palm as she sulked into his photo.

'Why couldn't you come along in ten years' time?' she muttered, twirling the mouse pointer over his delectable mouth. He was perfect. Both sexually and on paper. Her absolute Mr Right. Only she wasn't ready.

Her eyes slid to the family photo on her desk—Mum, Dad, her sister, her—all so happy. Especially her. She'd been leaving for university that day, buzzing with excitement over the future. No one could have known that twenty-four hours later her dad would no longer be with them. Taken too soon by a heart attack brought on by his determination to be everything to everyone.

And she'd made a promise—to herself and to him—that she would be the success he had dreamed of her being. That she would secure the future he had wanted for them all.

But she wouldn't make the same mistake and pursue it all at once—a successful career *and* a family of her own.

She wanted both, but a relationship, her own family—that could wait. She was only twenty-eight. She had time to wait for her financial circumstances and the company structure to be such that she could strike the right balance.

At least that was what she'd thought before her mum had got sick. Now she wasn't so sure of anything. Her tummy twisted painfully and she pressed her palms into the desk.

Get back to work...you're safe with work.

She looked at the computer screen and promptly closed down Mr Distraction. It was for the best. Losing herself in spreadsheets would help and she had work to do: financing the new product stream, sorting out resources...

Her thoughts trailed away, her eyes trailing with them, and the sight of someone exiting the lift across the office caught her eye.

It wasn't... It couldn't... What the fuck?

She catapulted out of her seat, knocking over her coffee in the process. The steaming liquid seeped across her desk, but she couldn't move, couldn't care. Her entire being was set on the man striding with absolute confidence towards her office—*Marcus!*

Excitement surged, her pulse tripped, and alarm bells resounded through her head as her best-laid plans sensed jeopardy. But he'd tracked her down, sought her out, and her heart swelled even as her stance hardened.

You can't have him.

The shrill ring of her phone jarred her. It was Anna. Blindly, she pressed the button. 'Not now.'

'But I have Tony on the line.'

Jennifer could sense the girl's frown, could see

her turn to look at her through the glass from her desk outside.

'He says it's urgent.'

She wasn't listening—not properly. 'Tell him I'll call him back. I have a visitor.'

'A visitor?' Anna's eyes left her to zone in on the man now only a few desks away. 'Right—a visitor. No problem.'

She was sure if she bothered to look Anna would be as transfixed by him as she was. Hell, everyone would be. He demanded attention.

But the only attention you're giving him is the been-nice-knowing-you kind.

Her tummy sank and she took a breath.

She could do this…

If someone had been riding his bollocks right now, Marcus didn't think he could have been any more uncomfortable.

Her eyes were on him. He could feel it. And, God help him, he couldn't even look in her direction. Andrews had been clear enough in his instructions. Out of the lift, across the foyer, through the rows of desks to the office straight ahead. That was where he'd find her.

And then the guy had pleaded. *'Let me speak to her first.'*

Like hell he was going to agree to that. The man had missed his chance. There was no way Marcus was going to let anyone but him deliver this news. He needed to do it, needed to make sure she gave him a chance to explain.

He paused at the desk positioned just outside her

office door and looked to the petite blonde sitting on the other side of it. She was currently doing something of a fish impression, a phone receiver hanging limp in her hold.

'Hi,' he said. 'I'm here to see Jennifer Hayes.'

'Uh-huh,' she said, making no effort to say any more or deal with whoever was on the other end of the line.

'Soooo…' he drawled, raising his brows and waving in the direction of the door. 'Can I go in?'

She didn't respond, but her eyes shifted to the office as the faint sound of the door opening reached him and sent every hair rising with the knowledge that she was approaching.

And then she spoke. 'Mr Wright?'

Take a breath…

'I think we can drop the "Mr", don't you?' he said, turning on his heel and feeling the hit of her beauty like a slug to the stomach.

He righted himself against it, adopting his faithful mask. The one that had got him through deal after deal. Only this time he questioned its success. The power of his reaction was so strong he was sure even her PA, who was still in full-on fish mode, was picking up on it.

'It's Marcus,' he said, putting one foot in front of the other and extending a hand, fixing his eyes on her face, not daring to lower his gaze, not wanting to see, but acknowledging all the same, the way the fabric of her green blouse clung distractingly close to her upper body. Or how the delicate length of her neck was accentuated by her hair being smoothed back and twisted into a severe knot high on her head.

Desire burned in his throat and he cleared it as her hand slipped inside his own.

She looked up at him, her crystal green eyes widening on a flicker of something—lust, nerves, fear… And then her hand closed around his and his blood rushed towards the contact, the softness of her palm doing things below the belt that he didn't want to permit.

He searched her face. *Did she feel it too?*

Her eyes glittered, streaks of colour shone through the make-up on her cheeks, and then her lips parted on a breath, the tip of her tongue flicking briefly across her lower lip. It was still there, the chemistry, he was sure of it. And the very idea that he could work with her and keep it platonic was fast becoming laughable.

But he would.

His no-mixing-business-with-pleasure rule existed for a reason. If only he'd been able to remember that last night, when he'd realised who she was, rather than letting her…

A flashback of racing images sent heat ripping through him and he coughed abruptly.

She started at the sound, her eyes narrowing on him. 'It's nice of you to come by,' she said, and then her eyes flitted about the room and saw their steadily growing audience. 'Do you want to go on in?' She gestured to her open doorway. 'I just need a brief word with my PA.'

'Of course.' He nodded and she stepped around him. He stared after her, teasing himself with the swaying curve of her hips, snug within a black pencil skirt.

For fuck's sake.

He snapped his eyes away and headed for her office. The sooner they could clear the air, the sooner he could focus on their relationship—their purely platonic, *business* relationship.

Entering her room, he was drawn to the bookcase running the length of one wall. Books were good. Books were calming. Books would get him in check.

He explored the titles, fingering the bindings— business, psychology, law... And then he paused, as a small collection tucked in the corner closest to the window drew his eye. He crouched and pulled one of the books out. He knew from the binding what he would find, and the entwined couple on the front only served to confirm it. He looked from the front to the back, scanning the blurb with a smile.

So the formidable Miss Hayes was a romantic at heart.

A throat was cleared directly behind him. *Shit.*

He looked at her over his shoulder. Her arms were crossed over her middle, her breasts bulging distractingly above them, and he tore his eyes away, slipping the book back into place and slowly getting to his feet to face her, his eyes carefully pinned above neckline.

'Sorry, it's an occupational hazard,' he explained. 'I like to understand people, and their books can give quite the insight.'

He smiled and watched her colour slightly, her eyes flicking over her little collection before returning.

She cocked a brow. 'Nosy, much?'

'What can I say? It pays to understand people.'

She surprised him with a laugh and, shaking her head, strode to her desk—just as her PA walked in, a roll of paper towel in her hand.

'Here you go,' the girl said, passing it to her. 'You sure you don't want me to do it?'

'Don't be silly—it's my mess.' She wrapped a fistful around her palm and tore it off. 'Thank you.'

'I'll let you get on, then.'

Her eyes flicked briefly in his direction before returning to Jennifer in a widened state. *Was this girl all together there?*

'Let me know if you need anything else.'

'Will do,' Jennifer said, her attention now fixed on the desk.

He followed her gaze to an upturned mug and a dripping mess. *How had he missed that?*

She righted the cup and started to mop at the liquid.

'Want some help?'

She gave him a brief look. 'You've done enough.'

Surprise made him chuckle. 'I'm not quite sure how to take that.'

She straightened, smoothing her free hand over her hair, and then she looked to him again, for longer this time—long enough for him to make out the pulse twitching in her neck and the re-emerging colour in her cheeks.

'Truth is, you gave me a shock when you came in and the coffee took the hit.'

'Ah.' He looked from her to the puddle. 'In that case, I'm definitely helping.'

He strode towards her, ignoring the flash of panic in her eyes, and held out his hand.

Reluctantly, she separated out some sheets and thrust them into his palm. 'You can do the floor.'

He smiled. Relegated to floor work? He could cope with that.

He could think again.

No sooner had he crouched down than he found himself face-to-face with her stiletto-clad feet.

Cope?

He'd be lucky to get back on his feet and keep his surging erection hidden.

Christ, but her ankles were hot, their delicate curves raising elegantly from shoes whose heels evoked desires so carnal and fierce they brought him to his knees.

And there he was, dropping forward, knees pressing into the hard floor as he began wiping at the puddle. It would be funny if he wasn't doing his damnedest to stay on task, trying not to get distracted by the shimmer coming off her legs, or the memory rampaging through his mind of how their stockinged lengths had felt beneath his palm. How it had felt to hook them over his hip and have her ride against his…

'Are you trying to polish a hole in my floor?'

He looked up to find her looming over him, her eyes burning into his own.

Christ, he wanted to bury himself between her legs.

Hell, if they weren't in her office perhaps delivering the news while driving her to climax would somehow take the edge off.

Yeah, real businesslike, that.

She was still looking at him, her eyes alive with some hidden thought, and he heard himself say, 'I like to be thorough.'

She gave a delectable little hum and nodded, muttering something that sounded very much like, 'Don't I know it?'

'What was that?' he said, rocking onto his feet

and tossing the dirty towels in the nearby wastebasket. His body was teetering dangerously close to the edge of reason.

'Nothing,' she blurted, her mood shifting so swiftly he wondered if he'd imagined her words.

It doesn't matter. Tell her. Now.

'Look, I—'

They both said it in unison.

'Jinx.' She gave him a smile that screamed regret. 'I'm flattered, I really am, that you've tracked me down and gone to all this trouble—it's lovely, it really is, and last night… Well, last night was probably the best—'

She was rambling. He knew it and she knew it, judging by the flush creeping up the exposed skin of her chest.

He tore his eyes upwards, forcing himself to look into her eyes as he cut her off. 'I'm not here because of that.'

She frowned. 'You're not?'

'Not entirely.'

Hell, just get it out. You've dealt with hostile takeovers better than this.

'I mean, I'm not here for what you think.'

Her brow furrowed further. Her genuine confusion was breaking him.

'Okay…' She threw her dirty paper towelling away, then returned her arms to her middle. 'So why *are* you here?'

He thrust his hand through his hair. The guilt, the alien sense of unease, the fear of hurting her—all made it impossible to think straight. He'd planned it out on the journey over, prepared his words, perfected

his apology, but it all evaded him now that she was
standing before him, waiting…

'Right.' The word was more for himself than her,
as his hands came up in a definitive gesture that said
Let's do this. 'There's no easy way to tell you what I
need to, so I'm just going to come out and say it. But
before I do you have to understand that when we met
I had no idea who you were.'

Her eyes narrowed. 'Well, why would you?'

'Because the business I told you I was in town
for…'

She nodded and he lowered his hands, shoving
them into his pockets.

'It was Tony Andrews I was supposed to be meeting.'

Her lips parted in surprise. 'Tony?'

'Yes.'

Her head gave a little shake. 'But why?'

'We were discussing this business…*your* business.'
He watched the confusion rain down over her face
and pushed himself onwards, ignoring the sinking
feeling in his gut, the sheer shittiness of what he was
about to tell her.

'My business?' She shook her head more fervently,
a lock of hair falling distractingly across her paling
cheek.

Stick with it, Marcus.

'But that makes no sense,' she said softly. 'Tony
hasn't mentioned any potential work with Tech-Incorp.'

She coloured slightly at the name, realising she had
revealed too much in that sentence. So she'd looked
him up? He would have been flattered if not for the
fucked-upness of it all.

'That's because it's not a simple joint venture.'

She brought one hand up to her mouth, her expression changing as he could see her putting it together, piece by piece.

'He was supposed to have spoken to you,' he continued, very much on the defence. 'In fact, he was supposed to bring you to meet me last night so we could discuss the future in a more relaxed environment.' He withdrew one hand from his pocket to rake it through his hair again, his prepared words coming back to him. 'He wanted the opportunity to explain his reasoning and make you understand why he was doing it. All before the paperwork was signed.'

'The paperwork?'

'He kept saying he wanted to tell you himself, and I've been pushing him for weeks to speak to you, but there's no telling that guy.' He shook his head with genuine frustration. 'Last night was his final opportunity and he couldn't even get *that* right.'

'His final opportunity?'

She looked lost now, as if she couldn't believe what she was hearing.

'Yes.' He pushed on. 'Time was of the essence. He needed the deal done this morning and it worked for me too.'

She came alive on a harsh laugh. 'It worked for *you*?'

Shit...

'Just to be clear,' she bit out, the hand in front of her mouth moving to slice the air between them. 'What *exactly* has he signed?'

He looked at her head-on. The woman who had driven this company to the fore was very much present now. Jennifer from last night was long gone. There was no carnal promise to her gaze, no flirtatious tilt to her mouth. Her countenance was like steel, cold and hard.

And that suited him just fine.

This Jennifer he could work with.

'He's sold his half of the business.' He rolled his shoulders and jutted his chin. 'To me.'

CHAPTER SEVEN

'You?'

Before her, Marcus nodded, the movement send-ing hair across his forehead with appealing charm.

He had no right to be appealing or charming. Not when she wanted to scream, to vent her anger and get to the bottom of what the hell had happened.

She'd been made a fool of. By the pair of them.

Betrayal clawed its way into her stomach, and nau-sea was instant and dizzying.

She'd been all out for anonymous sex—no names, no future, no nothing. And yet he—he had known. From the moment his driver had secured her name he had known who she was.

'I tried to stop things,' he said, as though reading her rampant thoughts.

'Yeah, you tried *really* hard,' she said, barely ac-knowledging the truth of his words, her fingers sweep-ing over her tingling cheeks.

'I tried to take you home to your place.'

She nodded. 'I remember.'

She remembered all too well. He'd tried and she'd pushed, seducing him until he'd bent to her will.

But she hadn't known. He had.

'I need you to go.'

'I think we should talk this through.'

She looked at him, her enlightened gaze seeing him clearly for the first time, and the fool inside her shrivelled and died. 'What? So you can lie to me some more?'

His eyes flashed. 'That's not fair. I didn't lie.'

'You lied by omission.'

She could see him struggling for an apt response, and his silence spoke volumes. Part of her wished he could smooth it over, make it all better, because the burn of humiliation was crippling her brain. She couldn't process any of it—his deceit, the dogged attraction to him she still shamefully felt, Tony's effing bail-out...

Christ—Tony!

The guy had truly surpassed himself this time. How could she have been so blind to his plans? And so trusting as to have delayed that sodding Shareholders' Agreement.

Such an idiot. That would have prevented it all, for heaven's sake.

But then, she'd never expected this. That he would actually jump ship and bring this potent heap of man trouble to her door.

It was a disaster.

An absolute fucking disaster.

'You need to leave.'

'Look, I understand that you're angry, and you have every right to be.'

'How big of you.' Inwardly she winced. She sounded like a disgruntled teen and she hated it.

'But the sooner we can put this behind us,' he

said, ignoring her little outburst, 'the sooner we can concentrate on the future and get our working relationship on the right footing. It's what's best for the business, after all.'

Words failed her. The more he spoke, the calmer he became, and all she wanted was to mirror that control. The fact that she couldn't made the situation a hundred times worse. And now he was using *her* business as a tool to reign her in.

Well, fuck that.

'What's best for the business is for me to understand Tony's motivation for leaving and get my head around your arrival. Then we can talk.'

He nodded, his expression one of annoying understanding. 'This afternoon, then? Or tonight? Over dinner, maybe?'

Afternoon...tonight...dinner...

She gave a manic laugh. 'Are you for real? You expect me to just roll over, take this news and pick up where we left off?'

'Hell, no!' he said, his eyes widening with what she could only read as horror. 'I want to talk business and strategy. Where and when doesn't matter to me. I wasn't suggesting a *date* of any sort.'

'Why?' she sniped. 'Does the idea suddenly seem repulsive to you?'

'Sorry, that came out wrong.'

He actually had the decency to look sheepish, and the change made him almost boyish. God help her if she didn't want to jump his bones as much as she wanted to kill him.

'I just mean it's not something I endorse. I have a rule never to mix business with pleasure.'

She stared at him incredulously. 'I repeat—are you for real?'

'Last night was different,' he stressed. 'Things had already gone way too far before I knew who you were.'

She clamped her jaw shut. *What the hell could she say to that?* By the time he'd discovered who she was she'd been like a dog on heat, and as for him... He'd been right there with her.

But still it didn't make it right.

She took a slow breath, smoothing a hand over her hair as she raised her chin and straightened her spine. This was happening, whether she liked it or not. The sooner she buried the emotional wreckage, the sooner she could deal with the professional fallout.

And that was all that mattered.

It had to be.

'Fine,' she said, purposefully shifting her attention to rifle through the papers on her desk. 'I'll have Anna clear my diary for tomorrow. We can meet then.'

She didn't look up, hoping everything in her tone and demeanour had delivered the dismissal he deserved. And yet he hesitated. She could feel his eyes still on her, the tension in the air still tight.

'What?' she suddenly blurted, her composure cracking as the need to goad him burst free. 'You can't wait until then to see me?'

Her gibe hit its mark, his eyes flaring. 'Very funny, Jennifer.'

'If you find this *funny*, I have serious concerns about your sense of humour.'

He looked as if he would say something else but stopped, his shoulders rolling on a heavy sigh. 'Look,

I know I've not done a great job of explaining myself, or the situation, but you must know that the sooner we get talking strategy, the sooner we can move forward and put this inconvenient start behind us.'

He studied her for a moment, probably waiting for a response, and when none came he turned and left, leaving her staring after him, the word *inconvenient* bouncing provokingly around her head.

Inconvenient?

Incon-bloody-venient?

The man was an arse!

She'd show him what *inconvenient* truly looked like.

Beneath her, her legs trembled against her bravado and her tummy turned. She was grateful she hadn't eaten breakfast that morning, because surely it would be making a return right now.

She could handle this. She just needed to break the problem down into two parts, or rather two men, and deal with each in turn.

First up—Tony.

Collapsing back into her chair, she reached out and pressed her index finger to the phone to dial Anna. She would know where Tony had been calling from. Anna wasn't just her PA, she was good friends with Tony's wife. And Jennifer would be damned if she was having this conversation with him over the phone.

She rapped on the door and fought the urge to test the handle. What she really wanted to do was rip the damn thing open and confront Tony wherever he stood.

She knew Lucy wasn't home. His wife had apparently given him a kick up the arse, taken the baby and moved out. For how long would be up to him.

Things were worse than Jennifer had realised. Worse than even Anna had understood.

Guilt cajoled her anger. *She should have realised.* If not for everything else on her plate, she probably would have. But bailing out of their company without a single word to her, bringing a total stranger into their midst—it felt like the ultimate betrayal.

Through the bevelled glass of the heavy black door she could make out his approach and she stepped back. Her eyes scanned the traditional London townhouse as she waited.

She heard the latch shift and looked to the door as it opened, Tony's head appearing at its edge. She swallowed back a gasp. He looked like hell. His blond hair flopped around his face, his eyes were glassy and sunken in their shadowed sockets.

'Jenny,' he rasped, eyes squinting, one hand holding a half-empty bottle of Jack Daniels and swinging it upwards to rest against the frame.

'You going to let me in?'

'You sure you *want* to come in?' His words were slurred and he looked towards the street, eyeing it up and down as though someone might be following.

'I don't think you want this particular conversation out here.'

He snorted and swung back, the door moving with him. 'Suit yourself.'

Jennifer stepped inside. Holding her breath against his alcohol-tainted air, she bypassed him and headed straight down the Edwardian-style hallway for the lounge.

He couldn't have been home alone for long—the house was too clean, too orderly. The high-ceilinged lounge barely looked lived in. All a marked contrast to his haggard state.

Tugging off her coat, she tossed it on one of the beige sofas but didn't sit. She wasn't ready to make herself at home. Instead she strode to the window, and waited until she heard him shuffle in behind her.

She tried to muster up the anger, the hurt, but as she turned to face him all she felt was sadness. He was pale and clammy, his white shirt hanging half open, his dark trousers out of place and a dramatic contrast to the pasty white feet sticking out beneath.

She took a steadying breath. 'I'm going to put the kettle on.'

'Suit yourself.' He swung the bottle and took a swig, wincing as he swallowed it down.

For fuck's sake!

She strode across the room and reached for the bottle. 'Let me get you a cuppa.'

His gaze dropped to her hand, his eyes wavering with the effort to focus. 'I'm good.'

'You'll be better with tea.' She closed her hand around the bottle and pulled.

He resisted, but only for a second, then his hand dropped away. 'Ah, Jennifer, you always know best.'

'And don't you forget it.'

She'd managed to inject a jovial confidence into her tone, but inside she was trembling, tears biting at the backs of her eyes. She needed to get away from him before she broke down.

'Go and sit down. I'll be back in a second.'

He slumped off to fall onto the nearest sofa and

Jennifer hurried into the kitchen, her shaky hands tapping on the kettle and reaching for mugs. She placed them on the worktop and pressed her fingers to her cheeks, breathing back the tears.

How long had he been this bad? Why hadn't she seen it?

She wanted the truth out of him—all of it—and she wanted it yesterday. But right now she'd settle for having the old Tony back. The one who had given her a career break and the backing that had got her where she was today. She'd forgive him everything and deal with whatever the future held for the company, for her, for Marcus…

The kettle bubbled with its impending boil, but its sound was broken by the shattering of glass.

What the hell?

She sped back through the house, her pulse racing. She entered the lounge just in time to see Tony hunching forward, reaching for the pieces of a broken photo frame at his feet.

'Wait.' She hurried over and squatted down before him. 'I'll take care of it.'

He didn't even acknowledge her as his fingers slipped the family photo from beneath the shards.

'What have I done?'

'Shh.' She rested her palm against his knee. 'It's going to be okay—you'll see.'

'How can it be?' he said on a shuddering sob, his distraught gaze crushing her. 'I've ruined everything. My work, my family…everything.'

'We can fix it… *I promise*,' she said, desperate to calm him. 'Here—put your feet up so I can clean this up.'

Silently he did as she asked and she fled to the kitchen, telling herself it *would* be okay. She would get him the help he needed, whether he was willing to accept it or not. Lucy would certainly support her.

And as for Marcus—what the hell did he think he was playing at? Entering into a deal with a man who clearly wasn't of sound mind?

Screw his charity work and his exemplary public profile—that son of a bitch had a lot to answer for.

And she would see to it that he did.

CHAPTER EIGHT

MARCUS PRESSED THE speed button, increasing the already punishing pace of the treadmill. Around him music blared, his breath was coming in hard grunts, sweat trickled down his body and still she was there, filling his mind, teasing his body.

He tore his T-shirt over his head, swiping it over his face and across his torso before tossing it aside. He wasn't stopping until he was free of her.

He'd tried telling himself it was business that was getting him worked up, that they needed to be talking strategy ASAP and ensuring they were on the same page.

But like hell was it business.

He'd tried to work, to concentrate on anything other than her, and yet she persisted. Her appeal still resonated through him long after he'd left her standing there.

It didn't matter that she was mad at him, that he'd screwed up and jeopardised their business relationship. His body simply didn't care.

And that was unacceptable.

He hammered the speed button once more, his frustration burning through him. He would exhaust her out of him if he had to. Whatever it took to get himself back under control.

His mobile's screen flashing in its rest caught his eye and he cursed. He didn't want to be interrupted. He wasn't ready to finish.

He checked the ID and saw it was his doorman. He wouldn't ring unless it was important…

Easing off the speed, he muted the music and put the phone on speaker. 'Yes?'

'Sir, I have Miss Hayes here to see you.'

'Miss Hayes?' He stopped the treadmill entirely.

'Yes, sir, would you like me to send her up?'

He felt his pulse kick rebelliously and thrust his fingers through his hair.

So what if she'd changed her mind? So what if she couldn't wait until tomorrow? So what if she'd tracked him down?

'Sir?'

'Yes.' He pulled sweat-slickened strands of hair off his forehead and met his own determined gaze in the mirror ahead. *Business. It's all about business.* 'Bring her up.'

He grabbed the towel slung over the machine and cut the call, launching his contacts list next. He scrolled through them, drying off his face as he headed into the foyer, his mind made up. He would deal with Jennifer and then he would go out on a date. He had options. Even if a suitable companion wasn't leaping out of his contacts just yet, he would find one.

He came to a stop before the mirror-finish lift doors, his semi-naked body reflecting back at him. *Should he chuck some clothes on?* He was hardly dressed for a business discussion, not on any level, but to hell with it—what did she expect, coming to his home uninvited? If the sight made her suffer half as much as he had already, then it would be worth it.

Grinning, he slipped his mobile into the back pocket of his shorts and took hold of each towel-end, casually leaning back against the wall as he waited.

The lift slid into place, its doors opening and presenting him with the doorman, who stepped back to allow Jennifer to pass. She froze mid-step, her mouth parting in that appealing way he had become fascinated with.

'Marcus?'

'In the flesh,' he said, spreading the towel-ends and straightening up, his eyes leaving hers to dismiss the doorman. 'Thank you.'

The guy nodded and pressed the button to close the doors behind her.

She wore the same clothes she'd been in earlier that day, overlaid by a long beige trench coat—the kind she could wear with nothing beneath when the need arose.

His cock twitched. *Just get through this. Fun can come later. And not with her.*

'So, to what do I owe this pleasure?'

She scanned him from top to toe, her cheeks heating, her eyes alive. And then she swallowed, a shutter falling over her expression as she stepped forward, closing the distance between them.

'Can you do something for me?' she asked softly, pausing an arm's reach away.

The word *anything* rushed to the tip of his tongue and he buried the crazy retort. 'What is it?'

She raised a hand to his chest, and the unexpected

touch sucked air into his lungs, holding it there as her fingers trailed down, spread out over his naked torso.

'Can't you guess?' she purred, her eyes following her fingers and her delicate touch sending ripples of pleasure straight to his defiant groin.

What the fuck?

He fought to keep his head clear, to remember his plan of action—*the sensible one.* 'Considering you couldn't wait to be rid of me a few hours ago—'

He broke off as her fingers met with the waistband of his shorts and he dropped his gaze, saw his cock swelling at her touch mere millimetres from where he desired it. His mouth dried up, and his well-exercised muscles turned rigid with anticipation.

'No,' he continued tightly.

Business. It needs to be about business. But, God, the desire to push her, to see how far she was going to go…

'You're going to have to enlighten me.'

She stepped closer, her eyes lifting to his mouth. 'It's you that needs to enlighten *me*,' she said, raising her hands to twine them through the ends of his towel and pulling him down.

He told himself to stop, to end it before things went too far, but his head still bowed. Her smell was invading his senses, her mouth beckoning.

God, he wanted her.

She was a hair's breadth away when the mood suddenly shifted, her eyes snapping to his as she shoved at him. 'You can start by telling me what the *hell* you're playing at.'

He stumbled back against the wall, surprise knocking him off-kilter. She was beyond angry—he could see that now. Her eyes were shooting daggers, her skin flaring like her hair.

'Hell, Jennifer.' He righted himself, fingers raking over his face, desire still burning through him, intensifying his confusion. 'Seems I should be asking you the same question—coming here, throwing yourself at me and—'

'No,' she cut in. 'That little scene was about making myself feel better for what you did to me. Make no mistake. I had no intention of following through.'

'Is that so?' He shook his head.

So it was payback?

It was about getting him back for the wrong she felt he'd done her. Hell, he could understand that, even respect her for it. But the rest...?

'You came all the way here just to tease me?'

'Absolutely not,' she said. 'There's plenty I wish to discuss with you.'

Plenty to berate him for, if her whole demeanour was anything to go by. And, hell, he deserved it. He knew he did.

'In that case, you'd best take a seat in the living room.' There was no way he was having this conversation half-clothed, or without a cold shower first. 'I'll join you in ten.'

'In ten?' She frowned. 'Where are you going?'

'To take a shower,' he said, adding, for his own devil-like amusement, 'unless you want to join me?'

Her cheeks flooded anew.

'No, I didn't think so.' He spoke for her. 'Look, I need a shower. You can either wait or you can leave and we'll do this tomorrow? It's up to you.'

With that he turned and walked away. His intent was to show her that he didn't care. In reality he needed to put distance between her and the erection still pressing painfully against his shorts. It was clearly slow at getting the message that he'd been played.

Jennifer stared after him, hands fisted at her sides, her head a mess as she struggled to rise above her warring emotions.

She'd been fuelled by anger. On the taxi ride over she'd plotted her attack, determined to tease him, catch him on the back foot, make herself feel better over his deceptive behaviour and then, when she was happy she had him, to pull him apart over his dealings with both her and Tony.

It had been a great plan.

She just hadn't factored in a semi-naked Marcus, all pumped and slick, so ripped and mouthwatering she'd hardly believed her eyes. But the reality had been there, and the sight had been enough to send her best-laid plans departing with the lift and her knickers wet through.

It was disgraceful. Add to that his ability to dismiss her so readily off the back of their little exchange and she was hopping mad.

She'd had him right where she'd wanted him. It had been visibly evident. His hardness had been pleading for more. And she'd take heart in that, if it wasn't for the fact that it had taken every ounce of her strength to thrust him away.

In spite of her anger, and her hatred for what he'd done to her, to Tony, she still wanted him. It was unforgivable, intolerable and totally undeniable.

She wanted to scream her frustration, but sense won out. There was no way in hell she would risk him hearing how much he got to her.

Tearing her eyes off his distracting rear, she headed for the living area, her heels clicking against the rich wooden floor.

She didn't dwell on the last time she'd been there. Then, she'd navigated it in the dark, her hands feeling their way, hot from their recent exploration of his body. A body she'd felt completely within her rights to explore, to enjoy, to devour.

What a fool!

She scrunched up her face, forcing out the memory. *It hadn't been her fault—she had nothing to be ashamed of.* And, striding forward, she entered the vast living space that ran off the foyer.

It was impressive, to say the least, its glass walls making the London skyline and its setting sun the perfect backdrop. A large cream L-shaped sofa dominated the room, its clean lines made inviting by various oversized cushions. Plush rugs adorned the floor, softening the hard wood throughout.

And in the corner, halting her appraisal of all else, stood an exquisite grand piano, gleaming in the accented lighting. It called to her, and she felt a bittersweet warmth pulling her back to another time and place.

She headed for it automatically, slipping her coat from her shoulders and dropping it over the sofa as she went. She reached out, her fingertips gliding over the sleek black top, following its curve with pleasing familiarity and pausing when she reached the key lid.

She itched to lift it. *Could she still play? Would she remember anything her father had taught her?*

She nibbled at her lower lip and raised the lid, her fingers dropping to toy with the keys. The notes resonated through the air and she glanced anxiously in the direction of the foyer.

Ah, hell, what did she care?

She needed *something* to do while she waited—anything to keep busy...

Slipping onto the bench, she tested out a melody, surprising herself with what she could remember, and a soothing calm seemed to be taking over as her fingers ran away with it.

She missed this. Maybe it was time she got a piano for her apartment. Inwardly, she laughed. It would never fit. She'd have to move. And even then it wouldn't be as beautiful as this one. Or the one that sat untouched in her Yorkshire home. She'd never transport that down here either. It wouldn't feel right. Even though it would never be played—not while her mum was still with them—it belonged there.

Her tune changed with her mood, and melancholy consumed her as she let it flow through her fingers.

She played and played, relaxing into the rhythm, losing sight of where she was—until the air became tight and an awareness rippled through her. Her fingers froze, her eyes shooting to the foyer.

How long he'd been there she had no idea, but there he was. Freshly showered, his damp hair curling around his face, he wore a grey sweatshirt that clung indecently to his upper body, and faded jeans. His bare feet were super-casual. All very laid-back and chilled, save for the man himself.

She swallowed.

His face was hard, set like stone, but his eyes—they blazed, and an emotion she couldn't read seared her across the room. Heat consumed her, swirling through her core as guilt swelled.

She slipped her fingers from the keys, folding them onto her lap. 'I'm sorry.'

There was a flicker of something—anger, pain, she didn't know—and then it was gone, his face turned away as he crossed the room, heading for a drinks cabinet that looked fit for an exclusive bar.

'Don't be—you play well,' he remarked.

There was no edge to his voice, no emotion. As if she'd imagined the whole thing. Except she hadn't.

'Can I get you a drink?'

'I really am sorry.'

Christ, why was she still apologising? He'd said it was fine. Only she didn't believe him...

'It's been a while, and when I saw the piano I couldn't resist.'

'It's fine.' He extracted a bottle and glanced over his shoulder. 'I was just surprised. I don't know many people who play.'

She rose and stepped out from behind the piano, her mind scrambling to get back to her purpose, to the reason she'd come. But her brain felt clouded with the memories, the pleasure of playing, and then him in all his appealing and confusing glory.

He turned and walked towards her, two glasses of red wine in his hands. He offered one out. It was presumptuous, but it was what she needed, and she took it.

'Thank you.'

He watched her lift it to her lips, then lowered his eyes briefly before returning them to lock with hers. It was fleeting, but she felt the trail of his eyes over her skin like the warmth of the alcohol gliding down her throat and her pulse skittered.

She looked away, needing to protect herself, to hide his effect on her, and she sensed him smile—*did he know what he was doing to her?*

'Why don't you take a seat?'

She bit back the ridiculous retort *I'd rather stand.* This wasn't going to be quick and easy—sitting made more sense. Even if it did appear too comfortable, too relaxed.

Feeling his eyes on her, she walked to the sofa with deliberate grace and perched at its edge, her glass cradled between her hands.

He followed, his fresh, clean scent washing over her as he passed by, dropping onto the sofa alongside her. He was far enough away that they didn't touch, but not so far that his scent didn't continue to tease her, its heady quality drying her mouth with a multitude of wants and desires.

None of which tallied with the reason she was here.

She took another sip, using the wine's soothing influence to urge her back on course.

Think of Tony.

Think of Marcus's deceit.

Think of all that is bad, for Christ's sake.

'So, are you going to tell me why you're here?' he said. 'Or am I going to have to tease it out of you?'

That did it, and his implication sparked an indignant fire that had her eyes spearing his. 'I'm surprised you can't guess.'

'I'd like to think you couldn't stay away from me,' he said, and she ignored the flutter in her tummy. 'But after that display it's clearly not the case.'

'At least you're not deluded.'

He cocked a brow, his smile soul-corrupting. *'Touché.'*

She considered him, all laid-back charm and charisma, and her internal warning sign flared. He was dangerous to her on so many levels. Either he was an utter bastard, or he was a man she could like… really like—

Like? Was she crazy? He'd near enough lied to her.

'How could you do it?'

He tensed, all trace of humour evaporating. 'Do what?'

'Sleep with me when you knew we'd have to work together? Let me do all manner of…' Her voice trailed away. Memories now tainted in shame burned her through and she looked away, taking another drink before she could speak again. 'How could you?'

'I really am sorry.'

'Sorry isn't enough,' she blurted, looking back to him with rising anger. It didn't matter that his apology sounded sincere—she needed more than a simple sorry. 'Did you not think about how it would make me feel? How mortifying it is to know you kept it from me? That you let me do all that, knowing we would have to sit in a *fucking boardroom together* and deliver a professional front?'

The knuckles of the hand holding his glass flared white—he was going to snap the stem if he wasn't careful. She almost wished he would. Red wine all over his pale furnishings was the least he deserved.

'I wasn't thinking,' he said quietly. 'The truth is, there's no excuse I can give for my behaviour.'

'So, you're not even going to try?'

'I don't think it'll help.'

'Let me be the judge of that.'

He studied her, long and hard, his eyes wavering. 'Okay, I'll give you my excuse,' he said eventually. 'So long as you assure me it won't affect us going forward.'

'*Affect* us?' She gave a small snort. 'It's a bit late to worry about that.'

Silently, he studied her, his inner battle written in his face, and then he hunched forward, his eyes flicking away, to return dark and brooding. 'The truth is, the moment you walked into that bar I was hooked.'

Her eyelids fluttered, along with her heart, but she kept herself steady, refusing to look away.

'When you returned my interest I would have moved heaven and earth to have you.'

She swallowed, and the warmth spreading through her belly now was nothing like shame as her defences took a direct hit.

'And, as I've already told you,' he continued, 'when I found out your identity I tried to stop things. But you can be very...*persuasive*...when you want to be.'

Her cheeks coloured. 'You still should have told me.'

'I know,' he admitted. 'And under any normal circumstances, with any other woman, I would have— could have. But with you...' His eyes trailed over her, a subtle crease breaking his brow. 'For some reason I couldn't. I couldn't even think straight. I couldn't think past what you were doing to me.'

'You expect me to believe a man like you is ruled by his penis?'

He flinched, his own cheeks streaking with colour.

Fuck his boyish charm, she thought. *Why did he have to do that?*

'Last night, with you, for the first time in my life I'm ashamed to admit I was.'

Fuck—what was he saying? That the attraction between them had been too strong to deny? That he'd never felt that way before?

Panic bubbled in her throat. *Wasn't that how she felt too?*

Or—her stomach twisted—*was he hoping that flattery would see him free of her wrath? Well, screw that.*

'Are you trying to flatter your way out of this?'

'No, I can assure you I'm not,' he said strongly. 'I'm not proud of my actions, and I'm angry for not keeping myself in check, but I can assure you I'll do my damnedest to keep myself in check from now on.'

She pressed her lips together, a confusing mix of emotions was raging within, disappointment hitting the crescendo.

Hell, she shouldn't be disappointed, she should be grateful.

She needed it gone—this attraction, the desire, the distraction…

But where was the off switch?

Even his questionable behaviour regarding Tony wasn't enough to rid her of it. Or maybe it was if his justification on that score was full of shit.

She grabbed at it like a lifeline. 'Fair enough, but what about Tony?'

His eyes widened, her change in topic clearly surprising him. 'What about him?'

'Well, from all I've read you're a man to be admired,' she said evenly, 'not one to be despised for taking advantage of a man not in his right mind.'

He frowned, and she could see her words had stung.

'Is that what you think I did?'

'I don't know what to think,' she admitted with a sigh. 'I only know that the broken man I saw today had no business signing your agreement.'

'He needed that deal.'

'Is that what you told yourself to make it all better?'

'Look, Andrews came to me with a sound offer and I took it,' he said. 'Whatever his personal situation, it didn't come into it.'

'But you must've known something wasn't right—that *he* wasn't right?' she flung at him, her desperation to paint him bad ringing through her words. Working with a man she disliked would be hard, but it would be doable. The alternative—she raised her drink and took a long, slow sip—didn't bear thinking on.

'I had my suspicions at the time,' he said truthfully. 'But I'm a businessman, Jennifer. I didn't get to this point in life by being all soft and understanding.'

'So you just took advantage?'

'No, I did not,' he snapped. 'Surely you can see that ultimately my involvement has given him a get-out? A chance to fix his mess?'

Her fingers trembled around the glass. She didn't want to accept his argument but felt it register all the same. 'It's not right. He should've come to me, not you.'

'What?' he said incredulously. 'Why do you think *you're* the one to help him out of this? Do you know how much money we're talking? How much it's taken just to keep a roof over his head and see off his creditors?'

'I would've been able to do something.' Even as she said it she realised it was nonsense, that Tony was in too deep for her alone to have given him enough. 'Now he has nothing.'

'Only if he chooses it to be that way,' he said softly, his anger disappearing as quickly as it had come. 'I've given him ample money to start afresh and get himself sorted out. Yes, I know he's not in a good place, but I've given him the best possible chance. What he does with that is up to him.'

His words silenced her, his logic doing away with every rebuke, rational or otherwise, save for the desperate. 'He still should have come to *me*.'

'Why?' He shook his head and placed his glass on the table, turning in his seat to give her his full attention. 'I just don't understand it. You've done enough for him already. From all the digging I've done, it's clear you're the brains behind this operation—you're the reason the company has done so well. What is it that Andrews has over you to make you care so much?'

Her head swam with his admiration of her even as her need to defend Tony was roused. 'You don't understand.'

'Then *make* me understand.'

'Tony's a good man—a *really* good man,' she stressed when she saw he would refute her. 'He's not just a business partner to me.'

His jaw clenched and he looked away. 'I see.'

'No, I don't mean it that way,' she rushed out, feeling her mutinous body getting high on the tension in his. 'Seriously, there's never been anything like that between us.'

Her impulsive need to reassure him riled her. Yes, it helped Tony's case, but she wasn't blind to the infuriating fact that she cared for Marcus's opinion.

Raising her chin defiantly, she said, 'Not that it's any of your business.'

His eyes locked with hers, their depths so fierce she had the wretched impulse to take her words back.

'You're probably right,' he said, 'but it pays to know exactly what I'm walking into.'

She fidgeted beneath his probing gaze, not liking the direction of their conversation. It was too private. Too personal. She wanted an out and it came swiftly, loaded with heat.

'Like you knew what you were walking into when you slept with me?'

He stilled, and his intensity was all the more severe for it. 'And I told you I couldn't think straight with you seducing me.'

Her lower belly contracted, cutting off her breath. The ache was instant and dizzying as the memory of those moments in the car flooded her. She tried to push it out, not to dwell, but she knew he was reliving it too, could read it in the flecks lighting up his gaze.

'We're digressing,' she said, her voice annoyingly elevated, and she looked away, staring at the calming piano in desperation, hoping he would get the message.

She heard him shift and her pulse skipped. *Was he reaching for her?*

'You're right,' came his level response. 'Let's get back to Tony.'

Surprise, disappointment—all manner of things she shouldn't feel washed through her and she chanced a glance his way. He'd settled back, drink in hand, one arm draped casually over the sofa-back.

Bastard—how did he do that?

She lifted her glass to her lips, using the drink for cover. Her voice wasn't ready—hell, her brain wasn't...

'What I was trying to say,' she said eventually, 'is that I've known Tony a long time and he's done a lot for me.'

He nodded his acceptance of that much and she continued on. 'We met at a university recruitment fair in my final year and I impressed him enough that he offered me a job before I'd even graduated. I guess he saw the potential in me, and the drive to make it big.'

'I'm sure he did. I imagine you were a force to be reckoned with even back then.'

She smiled slightly. *Was that how people saw her? How he saw her?*

'Perhaps,' she said, 'but I had my reasons and he understood them.'

'Reasons?'

She hesitated. Not many people knew her true motivation, but Tony did—and that was what it really boiled down to. 'It was more than just a desire to make something of myself. I *had* to be successful and Tony did everything he could to help me.'

'*Had* to?'

She took a breath and let it out with her next words. 'My father died when I left for university.' There she'd said it. It always killed her a little when she voiced it. But she needed him to know, to understand. 'He left behind me, my mother and my younger sister.'

'I'm sorry,' he said, his gaze softening. 'I take it you were close?'

She frowned. It was a strange question. He had been her father—of course they'd been close. But then... *Did he not have a father he was close to?*

'Very,' she said, burying the thought—*she didn't need to know that about him*. 'No matter how busy he was, he always made time for us—in fact, he was the one who taught me to play.'

She gestured to the piano, a brief memory of being sat down with her father the Christmas he'd had it delivered filling her mind, and she gave a small smile, the gesture falling as the emptiness of him no longer existing returned.

'What happened?'

She met his eyes and something inside her cracked, his interest blindsiding her with the urge to cry.

'A heart attack.' She swept a hand across her dry cheek, smoothing away phantom tears. 'It was a long time ago, but it was unexpected. I guess the shock has never quite left me.'

He nodded with understanding. 'And so you do it all for him?'

'In some ways,' she acknowledged. 'He effectively ran himself into an early grave, making sure we had everything we could possibly want. And when he went… Let's just say things weren't too straightforward financially. My family home costs a small fortune to run and my mother isn't well. She needs a lot of support and living at home helps keep her settled…'

Thoughts of her mum had sadness welling up inside her, and she broke off as the helplessness of their situation sucked at her resolve and she felt exposed, too vulnerable, the tears too close to the surface.

'Your sister and mother both depend on you?'

She shrugged. 'I'm the breadwinner. My sister's due to start university next year, so there is only me, but I want to do it. I love my career, and I want to keep my father's promise of a good life for us all. I want to do him proud.'

'I think you've done that in spades.'

She smiled. 'You'll understand why I'm so indebted to Tony, then?'

'I wouldn't go that far.'

'*I* would,' she said, tears now forgotten with the acute need to make him understand. 'Seriously, it never would have happened without him. You didn't know Tony back then—how amazing he was, how he could read a situation or an opportunity so well and make the perfect call. He could handle people and business deals with such skill that it left us all in awe, and he taught me so much.'

Marcus nodded, decent enough not to argue, but she could tell he wasn't convinced.

'It's only in recent years that he's started to be so—' She broke off, unable to label it.

'Unreliable?' he provided for her.

She nodded ruefully. 'But after seeing him today

I'm beginning to understand it all. The gambling, the poor investments… I just had no idea he'd got himself into this bad a state.'

The shock of seeing him hit her anew and she shuddered. Her wine sloshed in her glass but she was too lost in the memory to care.

'It was soul-destroying to see him so out of it. So *drunk*. I mean, he looked *ill*. Properly ill.'

He reached out and took the glass from her shaky hold. 'He's an alcoholic, Jennifer. What would you expect him to look like?'

She froze. 'Don't be ridiculous.'

'I'm not.'

'I don't think getting off your face on the day you sell your share of your own business to cover a multitude of gambling debts and keep a roof over your family's head labels you an alcoholic.'

He studied her, his eyes searching.

Did he think she was lying? Covering up on Tony's behalf? Or in some strange denial?

'I'm serious. I know he has a gambling addiction and needs help—but an *alcoholic*?'

He leant forward to set his drink down and angled his body towards her. 'If it was a one-off I'd completely agree with you, but it's not.'

'What makes you say that?'

'From what I've seen, and heard on the grapevine, I believe he's been hitting the bottle for quite some time.' He rested his elbows on his knees and linked his hands together. 'The gambling is just another of his vices.'

'But I would *know* if he had a drink problem,' she said. 'He wouldn't have been able to hide it from me.'

'It's amazing how well it can be hidden.'

'But he didn't *say* he had a problem—not in that regard. He spilled his all to me today, but…'

'He probably doesn't even realise it himself. High-functioning alcoholics like Andrews often don't.'

Jennifer racked her brain, thinking over the times she had seen Tony of late. Had he ever been without a drink nearby, even at the office? His mood swings, his irrational behaviour, his forgetfulness… And then there were the cold sweats, when he'd told her he'd simply been unwell. Had that been something else entirely?

'Have I really been so preoccupied that I've totally missed the signs?' she asked, her voice distant, the truth of the situation and the magnitude of her failure as a friend setting in. 'I mean, Christ, he's given me so much and I've repaid him by—what? Not even *noticing*? Neglecting him when he needed me the most—not giving him the time—'

'Stop it, Jennifer.' He reached out and cupped her hands in his, the warmth of his touch contending with the chill running through her. 'Look at me.'

She did as he asked, her eyes meeting the fervent heat of his own.

'None of this is your fault,' he said. 'He has done this to himself. *He* is the one to blame—*he* is the one who has hurt those around him and let them all down. Not you.'

The bitterness in his voice cut through her. He made it sound so detestable, so personal…

'You talk like you're speaking from experience.'

His hands flexed around hers, his eyes flashing with a pain so raw that her heart clenched and her own problems—Tony's problems—temporarily faded.

'Are you?'

He blinked, his gaze falling away. 'Am I what?'

'Speaking from experience?'

A warning bell rang, but the question was out anyway, and the need to know rose from a part of her she couldn't ignore.

CHAPTER NINE

HE'D ASKED FOR THAT—her question.

He should have been more prepared, more composed. But seeing her break down, listening to her talk about her family, her responsibilities, and then having the whole Tony situation piled on top had thrown him off guard.

And then there was his guilt. *Christ*—now that he knew how much rode on her career... and along he'd come, shaking it up with his out-of-control cock.

What an arsehole.

And now he'd made another blunder—giving her a glimpse of the demons that no one had any business knowing about. No one saw that side of him. Not ever. He'd learned the hard way that emotions were for the weak, and that wearing them on your sleeve earned you a fist or worse.

But he looked to her now, and suddenly his philosophy no longer applied.

Her emotional tirade hadn't made her weak. It had made her beautiful—admirable, even—and the need to pull her towards him was killing him. He wanted to take away her pain and his past with the passion that flared so readily between them.

'You don't have to tell me,' she assured him softly.
'Not if you don't want to.'

Over her hands, his thumbs caressed her skin and
for a split-second he considered doing it—silencing
her with his mouth, making her forget it all.

And what would that make him?

An even bigger fucking arsehole.

He released her hands and dropped back into the
sofa, arching his neck over the back of it as he looked
to the ceiling.

If sex was out, what was left? More of the truth?
Didn't he owe her a little after all she'd told him?

'My father was a drunk.'

The words resounded around the room, out before
he'd even mentally agreed to them, the spoken confession so strange and alien.

'Your father?'

He flicked his eyes over her, taking in her sympa-
thetic beauty and wishing he'd buried his decency and
gone for sex. It would be easier now that she knew
who he was. Less complicated.

And that in itself was ridiculous. He had his rules
for a reason: business and sex didn't mix. And yet
letting this personal exchange continue felt far more
threatening.

'You don't need to listen to this.'

'I want to,' she said, leaning towards him, her palm
coming to rest on the sofa between them, her compassion filling the air.

Christ, she was good.

And he didn't have to tell her everything—just
enough to make her feel he'd shared...

Resigned, he glued his gaze to the perfectly

smooth white ceiling and linked his hands together behind his head. 'My father wasn't like Andrews,' he began, matter-of-fact. 'He was what you'd call a chronic severe alcoholic—one who liked to take his anger with the world out on me and then use alcohol as an excuse.'

'My goodness—that's awful,' she rushed out, her obvious horror making it impossible for him to overlook the brutal truth of his confession, of his past.

But he wanted to. He wanted to forget it all save for the lessons it had taught him.

The hairs prickled on the backs of his arms and he clasped his hands tighter. 'It is what it is.'

'Was he always that way?'

'No,' he acknowledged, his stomach drawing tight as the chill continued to spread under his skin. 'He was a Welsh miner. Life was tough, but he did all he could. He worked hard and he was well liked.'

Memories he didn't want pushed to the surface, telling him of happier times—of Christmases, birthdays, *eisteddfods*, picnics in the park; all three of them happy and content. And then…

'Everything changed when I was eight. My mother got sick, and by the time they detected the cancer it was too late. She was gone within a year.'

He felt Jennifer's touch before he sensed her move—felt her hand curving over his thigh and soothing the chill directly beneath.

'Oh, Marcus, I'm so sorry.'

He gave a forced shrug. 'Dad never recovered. He hit the bottle hard and never came back from it.'

'And he beat you?'

She sounded dazed, and her fingers were starting

to move over him in a gentle caress. He looked to her hand and then to her face. *Was she even aware she was doing it?*

'He was angry,' he said simply.

'But still…'

Her eyes watered and he snapped his own away, fixating on the ceiling.

'It was hell for a while,' he admitted after a pause. 'But when I turned twelve my grandparents took me in. I was a scrawny misfit who'd borne enough bruises to make people aware of what was happening and they couldn't sit by any longer.'

'Did you live with them for a while?'

'A few years,' he said. 'Long enough for my gran to teach me how to play the piano.'

His head rocked to one side, his eyes resting on the piano and bringing to him the evocative memory of Jennifer playing. She had been so beautiful, lost in the music—and, *fuck*, it had hurt like hell. Memories of his mother doing the same were thrusting his past in his face, pulling him apart with love and loss.

This was why he didn't let people in. This was why he shouldn't be letting her in now.

'How sweet.'

'Sweet?' Christ, he actually smiled, her choice of words sucking him out of the darkness descending. 'I'm not sure Gran would agree. Teaching a grumpy teen something as uncool as the piano came with its own challenges.'

She gave a small laugh, and her amusement lifted him further.

'I bet!'

'But what can I say? She knew what she was doing.

I was so full of angst and in need of an outlet for it. When sport simply ended in fist fights she opted to give me a more solitary hobby—even if I wasn't so keen in the beginning.'

'She sounds like a brave woman.'

'Or simply stubborn,' he said. 'When she puts her mind to something there's no stopping her, and she was determined that I should have something of my mother in me.'

'And so you should.' The emotion caught in her voice as she squeezed his leg. 'It's a lovely thing she did. I'm sure your mum would have been very proud.'

Lovely. Proud. He needed to get a grip on the situation. There was so much sentiment flying around he was starting to wonder where the real him had gone.

'Are your grandparents still around?'

He nodded, his gut knotting as thoughts of them in the present brought a new kind of pain.

'Do they still live in your home town?'

'Not the same house,' he said distractedly. 'I helped them secure a little cottage a few years back—close enough to the amenities but away from the hustle and bustle.'

'Do you see them often?'

'As often as work permits.' *Liar.* The knot in his gut twisted and turned with rising guilt. *But going back—it was so fucking hard.* 'Not as much as I should, I guess.'

'And your father—where's he?'

Dad. Christ!

His nails pierced the backs of his hands and his breath left him on a rush.

Her fingers above his leg froze. 'Sorry. I shouldn't—'

'He's dead,' he cut in over her. 'He died not long after I left home.'

'I'm sorry.'

'I'm not,' he said, sending her a look and seeing nothing but shock reflected back at him.

Hell, what did she expect? But then, what could she know about it? She'd been lucky enough to grow up safely ensconced in the love of her family, whilst he...

He quit the thought. His sudden anger was irrational—especially when it was directed at her, and especially when she'd been through her own kind of hell, losing her father and now her mother's sickness.

Fuck, he was a mess. In a pent-up state of hurt and need. And that *was* her fault.

He needed this over with now—before he did something stupid...desperate, even. His earlier battle came back to haunt him as his eyes flitted to those parted lips and he thought about what he'd threatened do. Before she'd coaxed the tale of his past out.

Don't do it. Sex is sex. You can get it anywhere. You can't get another her.

As much as the last thought came as a warning— *keep the business safe*—it also rang true for his bed. He wanted no one else.

'It's getting late,' he said tightly, aware of her fingers still upon his thigh and no longer finding her touch soothing or comforting. Far from it. They were urging on the part of him that still felt cheated and aroused by her earlier ploy.

But she deserves better than you... She pushed you away... Take the not-so-subtle hint.

Leaning forward, he reached inside his pocket for his phone. 'I'll give Colin a call and get him to take you home.'

'Home?'

It wasn't the first time she'd said that to him in that almost indignant tone, but what was she after this time? Did she want more misery out of him? Or was she after something else far more appealing, far more on his wavelength?

Don't be an idiot. Only fools make the same mistake twice.

'I think it's time we called it a night.'

He stood and took their wine glasses to the drinks cabinet while his mind refused to play ball. It was teasing him with a multitude of possibilities, all of which heated up as he heard her move, closing the distance between them.

His back prickled with rising awareness but he refused to turn. He set the glasses down, purposefully avoiding her as he looked at his phone and unlocked it.

Just a few minutes. He just had to hold out long enough to get Colin.

'Wait,' she said, her voice so close, so coaxing.

Don't wait. Just do it.

'I'll just—' He broke off as she reached around him, his body coming alive as her hand smoothed over his, and then he felt the phone shift, slipping out of his hold as she took it from him and set it down next to the glasses.

'Don't, Jennifer.' He tried to step away but there

was nowhere to go. Between her and the cabinet he was locked in.

'I'm really sorry.'

Sorry? She was sorry?

He twisted his head in surprise, getting her in his peripheral vision but not daring to focus. 'You have nothing to apologise for.'

'I do if I've upset you.'

'Don't be crazy.'

He turned to her with the ardent need to reassure and realised his mistake too late, the brush of her body against his front sending all hell breaking loose inside.

He breathed through it, thrusting his hands into his pockets. 'I'm the arse in all of this.'

'As much as I want to agree...' Her smile was small and wavering, and her eyes lit on his mouth a moment too long before returning to his. 'I can see I've upset you enough to want me gone, and I'm sorry for that.'

'Christ, Jennifer, this isn't about you upsetting me.'

Her eyes searched his. 'It isn't?'

She was so close. It would be so easy.

He let go of a ragged breath, his eyes lost in the intense green of hers, and he spied the moment it dawned on her, her breath catching, her teeth dragging in her bottom lip. The gesture was nervous and endearing and sexier than it had a right to be.

'Do I really need to spell it out for you?' he asked as she stayed quiet, and she nodded, all innocent and curious and purposely teasing.

He shoved his hands in deeper, imprisoning them.

'Don't do this, Jennifer. Don't let me go back on my word.'

'Your word…?' she pressed softly, releasing her bottom lip and leaving it distractingly slick.

He forced his eyes away. 'I told you I'd keep myself in check.'

'You told me you'd try your hardest.'

Fuck, show some mercy.

'I did, and that's why you should go.'

'I know what I *should* do…but…' She looked at him, eyes wide with desire, and his body reacted in kind.

Shit.

He took hold of her hips, intending to turn her away, but the delicious heat permeating through her skirt killed his intent. 'Please, Jennifer, you need to help me.'

'I can't,' she said, and for a second he saw her own uncertainty, her own confusion. 'I don't know what it is… Maybe it's the fact I've shared more with you tonight than I ever would normally.' She shrugged. Her eyes, bright with honesty, flitted to his lips and back again as her hand closed around the base of her throat. 'I just feel so open, exposed…raw, almost…'

'You and me both,' he said, realising the truth of it, knowing it should bother him and not caring all the same.

'Maybe it's that you're forbidden territory now…' She cocked her head to the side and studied him, a kind of confidence coming over her as she seemed to shift gear. 'Or maybe it's simply the fact I feel cheated—that you fucked me knowing exactly who I was, whilst I…'

Her words trailed off, her eyes burning into his and sucking him in completely.

Do it. You know you want to. Screw sense.

'And if we do this,' he said, 'then what? We just act like it never happened afterwards?'

Her hands slid up his chest, brushing over his pecs, curving over his shoulders. A trail of crazed sensitivity erupted in their wake as she nodded.

'Exactly.'

His fingers flexed against her hips. The desire to lift her, carry her to the sofa and do all manner of things raged through his brain. But he needed to hear her say it. He wanted there to be no risk of misunderstanding, no risk to their business relationship.

'So, what are you saying?'

'That I need a chance to get you out of my system,' she said, holding his eyes, 'to have sex with no lies. You can see it as an IOU, if you like.'

An IOU? Christ, had she really just said that?

'One night?' he pressed, bowing his head.

She hooked her fingers around his neck, loving how his heat permeated her fingers, how the scent of his recent shower engulfed her.

Yes, an IOU—a night to burn him out of her. But would it work?

Doubt nagged, but she didn't care—not with this crazy need building that only he could slake.

She raised herself on tiptoes and felt his breath catch as she paused, lips hovering a hair's breadth from his.

'Just…' she tugged on his lower lip '…one…' she flicked her tongue out to tease his upper lip '…more…'

she pressed her bottom lip against his parted mouth
'…night.'

'Fuck, Jennifer,' he growled, thrusting his hands
into her hair and crushing her mouth with his, his pos-
session wild and feverish and everything she craved.

'Yes…' she moaned into his mouth, her fingers biting into his neck as she sought to keep them together,
fearing he would back away, would change his mind,
return to his earlier plan and get Colin.

*Fuck Colin—there was no way she was leaving.
Not yet.*

Desperately she dropped her hands to the hem of
his sweatshirt, wanting it gone, needing him bare to
her touch. She scrabbled it up his chest, felt his hands
manoeuvre to do the same to her blouse, to pull it out
of her skirt. She heard the faintest sound of tearing—
his top, her blouse? She had no idea. She didn't care.

'That was Armani, you know.' He chuckled against
her, breaking his mouth free only long enough to deliver the words.

She ripped her own mouth away. 'I couldn't give
a fuck.'

'You will soon.'

He claimed her mouth again, his fingers working
at the buttons of her blouse, and a frustrated sound
gave way at the back of his throat.

He pressed her away, glaring down her front. 'I
hate buttons.'

And then his hands were on the parted fabric
and he yanked at it hard, the buttons flying free as
she gasped, his impatience flooding her belly with
an excited rush as the fabric fell loosely around her
shoulders.

His eyes burned into her exposed body. 'I'll buy you another.'

She shook her head. 'I think it makes us even.'

She tugged his sweatshirt over his head and he took advantage of the move, bowing his head to her upper body as she pulled the sleeves from his arms, administering kisses, nips and sucks. His hands kneaded her above her bra, his attention urgent and driving her crazy. She tossed his top aside and forked her fingers through his hair, holding him against her.

'Yes—God, yes!' she cried, and he spun her, twisting away from the cabinet and bringing her up hard against the wall. She threw her head back into the hardness, her eyes closed as tension built like wildfire.

His fingers slipped around her back, finding the fastening to her skirt and doing away with it, shoving it down her legs. His head lowered with the move, down to the valley between her breasts, to her undulating belly, until his heated breath was sweeping her panties.

She felt his fingers flick open each suspender, his touch gently coaxing as he circled her thighs with each move. Her legs quivered with the thrill. And then his mouth was back, tracing a path down one leg as he slipped off one shoe and stocking and repeated the move with the other.

He was sending her clit into a frenzied state of need. Her wetness was slipping between her thighs, her whimpers heedless, her words nonsensical as she heard herself pleading with him to do something... *anything*.

And then his mouth answered, his tongue probing above her knickers, and she bucked into it, shamelessly riding his face in desperation. His hands slid up her hips, hooking beneath the lace of her thong and tugging it down.

It dropped to her ankles and he cupped one thigh, coaxing it over his shoulder, forcing her to use him and the wall for balance and part before him. And then his mouth was upon her, his tongue hitting the nested nerve-endings that were so desperate for him, and she lost sight of everything except the tension coiling through her limbs.

'You taste so good,' he rumbled against her, his fingers slipping up to tease against her opening. 'So wet.' He sucked on her clit and she bucked wildly. 'So ready for me.'

He slid his fingers inside and the need to have him fill her, to have him inside her when she came, had her fingers clawing into his shoulders.

'Marcus, fuck me.'

'We have the whole night for that.'

'But I want you in me,' she rushed out. 'Please, Marcus, *now.*'

He groaned, unhooking her leg as he shot to his feet, his hands moving roughly to her hair as he pulled her head back and locked their gazes together.

'You have no idea what those words do to me, coming from your lips.'

She hooked her leg around him and pressed herself against his hardness. 'I can feel what it does.'

He gave a jagged breath and she felt the rough seam of his jeans biting into her sensitive clit as she wriggled into him, finding her spot, finding a rhythm that soothed and built.

He released her head, his hands falling to curve

around her hips, his eyes lowering to watch as she rode against him, and then he rasped, *'Condom.'*

She gestured to the sofa. 'My coat, my purse…'

It took a moment for her meaning to hit and then he swept away, back in seconds, her coat in his hand. She took it from him, shaking with pent-up need as she forced her hands to do her bidding, locating her purse, extracting the packet and tossing the rest away.

He was back with her, his body pressing her against the wall, his hands lifting her thighs around him, his mouth hot and urgent as he devoured her lips, her neck, the heated flesh above her bra. She didn't need more teasing…she needed him filling her—now.

'Marcus,' she pleaded, pressing against his chest, feeling his skin burn into her fingers. *'Now.'*

He raised his head, eyes ablaze as he straightened and lowered her legs. He moved to take the condom and she lifted it, holding his eyes as she locked her teeth around the perforated edge, freeing her hands to undo the button fly of his jeans.

His cock sprang free against her, and his bareness was both surprising and exhilarating as she slipped her hands around him. 'Commando?'

'I was in a hu—'

His words died on a hiss as she pumped him, the slickness over his tip telling her he was close, and she smiled up at him.

'Don't,' he groaned, his hands flying to the wall either side of her, muscles flexing, jaw clamping shut, the pulse working furiously in his neck.

So close.

Her thighs clenched, the ache painfully acute as she tore the packet open and took out the condom, one hand holding him tight at his base, the other rolling it down, taking her time, enjoying the way his jeans hugged tight over his hips, his cock protruding above, so big, so hard for her.

Her eyes shot to his face in fascination. His hands weren't even on her and the tension still built. Her body was getting off on his visible fight to keep contained, his eyes glazed with need, every muscle rippling with tension. Fuck, he was beautiful, in every which way, and she wanted him with every ounce of her being.

It should scare her.
It would scare her.
But not now.

Reaching his base, she squeezed, and he reacted instantly, his hands flying to her wrists, drawing them up and away, pinning them above her head as he pressed her back against the wall.

'You enjoy torturing me.'

She bit into her lip, the desire raging through her system making it impossible for her to respond.

He imprisoned her wrists in one hand, his other coming down to take hold of his cock, lowering it down her belly. Instinctively she raised herself on tiptoes, desperate to get him where she wanted him.

'My turn,' he said, bending his knees, sliding his hardness between her legs, rocking teasingly against her clit, across her opening but not inside.

His gaze burned down to where their bodies met, and hers did the same, watching as he moved back and forth, back and forth, the condom slickening with her need.

'Please…' She sounded pained, the desperation too much to bear, and she writhed over him. *'Fuck me.'*

He cursed, the noise primal as he released her wrists, shifting both hands to grab her thighs up and around him, getting her steady before freeing one hand to position himself at her entrance. And then he thrust, so hard, so deep, he filled her instantly.

'You feel so damn good,' he said, withdrawing before plunging once more, the move slow and sure.

Her blouse was tangled up in his fist, pulling tight over her arms, restricting her, pushing her onwards and upwards. She worked with his thrusts, sparking off a frenzied rocking fuck that had her tension spiralling out of control, the position offering up the perfect friction, the perfect everything.

It was so good.

So right.

She was flying, her entire being swamped by pleasurable heat, and then she shattered over him, head thrown back, lids clamped shut. She wanted to ride the wave for ever, to draw it out…

And then her ears were filled with his guttural groan, and the buck of his lower body was telling her that he was gone, his head falling forward to press into her shoulder, his arms around her bulging taut. She clenched him inside her, wanting to hold him, keep him there, loving how he pulsed inside her, how his entire body trembled its release. It was so sexy, so beautiful, and pain ripped her apart.

She didn't want to give this up. She didn't want to give him *up.*

She shut her eyes and pressed a kiss into his shoulder, pushing it all out. It didn't matter what she wanted. It wasn't possible. It wasn't sensible. It wasn't right.

And yet as she listened to their elevated breaths, felt their bodies relax with sated need, something shifted deep inside her.

The tight hold she'd always had over her life, that kept everything heading in the right direction, no longer felt so tight.

CHAPTER TEN

MARCUS HIT THE shower, its spray veering on cold.

She'd gone again. Left before morning. But no note—no handwritten *thank-you*. This time he'd got an email, asking that he review the attachments enclosed before they got together later that day.

Her message was clear: all work from here on in.
Hell, it was your message too, remember.

So where was the sense of relief? The clear head that was supposed to accompany the morning after?

The moment he'd realised she was gone a punching great weight had settled in his stomach. It had to be disappointment. The realisation that he'd had his last of her, that there would be no morning goodbye. If he'd known he would have kept her awake for longer, savoured that last session all the more—the way her face had flushed, her body had glistened, her breasts had bobbed as she rode above him…

Heat seared him through, his cock stiffening with maddening intent.

He raised his head to the cold jets, fingers thrusting through his hair. He did not—*he would not*—get himself off. He hadn't needed to in years, and he wasn't about to start now. Christ, he'd come enough times already, so what was his fucking problem?

Looking for distraction, he forced his mind to the email she'd left him with and the attachments that detailed her vision for the company's future, as it had been before he'd come along.

It included a presentation she'd delivered to the workforce the previous day. Notably, Tony Andrews had appeared alongside her own name in the slides, suggesting it was supposed to have been a joint delivery. He'd obviously left her in the lurch with that too.

His fingers ground into his scalp. Why did he care so much? And what did it matter now? Andrews had gone, and things would be very different from here on in.

She had him.

Snatching the soap, he lathered himself up and ignored the peculiar way those words played with his mind. He had far more important things to think on—like the morning ahead.

He'd called a meeting for ten-thirty, bringing together the UK-based heads of product development from both companies. He hoped Jennifer would join them, but either way it was going ahead. They had no time to waste.

His Stateside head of marketing had emailed the previous evening, calling multiple times thereafter because he wanted to deliver some critical news.

Had he noticed? *Had he fuck!*

He'd been far too busy wrapped up in what he'd felt to be far more pressing at the time—*her.*

This *never* happened. He answered his phone, checked his email, did whatever work demanded. He was on call twenty-four-seven, as befitted his multi-national corporation and its time zone stretch.

Always available. Always at hand.

Until now.

Until… *Jennifer.*

He slammed the shower off and stepped out, grabbing his towel and drying himself off. It was time to move on.

Now they had a potential product launch in jeopardy because a competitor was about to pip them to the post. And, yes, he might be confident that their product would be better, but being the market leader didn't ring true when you were second out of the sodding gate.

He should have been holding a conference call while he and Jennifer had been *getting-to-know-one-other.* His lapse in focus meant he now had to wait for sun-up in the US to discuss the issue with his marketing expert.

Needless to say, he wasn't going to hang around.

He had a plan brewing.

He'd picked through Jennifer's business strategy, studied the organisational structure, current projects and existing priorities. There was an opportunity to save the situation if they moved quickly enough.

But still the feeling of chasing his tail persisted, and it bugged the hell out of him.

He tossed the towel aside and strode into his bedroom, dressing in a dark suit, a white shirt but no tie. His throat was already constricted enough.

He raked his hand through his hair, absentmindedly scanned his reflection and headed for the door.

It was time to get down to business.

Pure. Business.

* * *

Jennifer checked her mobile for the umpteenth time, one foot tapping impatiently as she waited for the lift to reach her office floor.

He had to be shitting her.

It was unsettling enough having him join the company unannounced, but to call a meeting like this without waiting for her, to take such an impudent step on his first real day, was taking the piss.

And she was later returning than she had intended.

Lucy's need to talk had been evident in her honesty that morning. Jennifer had managed to give her some reassurance, promising to get her husband the help he needed, and seeing the strain in the woman's face ease, even just a little, had been worth every delayed second.

Or so she'd thought.

It was pushing lunchtime now, which meant the meeting was in full swing.

And without her...

Frustration bubbled up her throat and she forced it down. She needed a level head to deal with the situation appropriately—*professionally.*

Finally the lift doors opened and she stepped out, faltering mid-stride as she spied Tony's office—in use. Its new owner leaned back against the glass wall, his arms folded, one leg crossed over the other, totally relaxed as he gave Maxine—her head of product development—his full attention.

Her petite, feminine charm shone across the distance as she stood at a flip chart and spoke to the room. There were two other attendees, both men she didn't recognise—likely part of his product development team judging by the invitation he'd sent her.

Jennifer was starting to draw looks from the staff and, forcing a smile, she put her legs in motion and headed over to Anna. 'How long have they been in there?'

'A couple of hours,' she admitted. 'Can I get you a coffee?'

'Please.'

She speared Marcus through the glass. Seeing him so at home, straight off the back of her morning's dealings with Tony's wife, only compounded her anger. Yes, he'd cleared himself of any wrong-doing in the business deal, but it didn't make seeing him in his predecessor's shoes any easier.

And then he turned his head, his eyes meeting hers, and defiant sparks of delight shot through her.

She looked away and strode straight into her own office, closing the blinds to shut him out as her anger swelled.

You're not angry at him for Tony's sake. You're angry because you can't control how you feel about him and you're angry because he's called a meeting that's pissed you off and still you want him.

She threw her coat over the stand and headed to her desk, extracting her mobile from her bag to check the meeting invitation. Double-checking, triple-checking that she'd declined it.

Sure enough, she had, and her response had made clear that it should be rearranged. A meeting entitled Product Prioritisation made her presence mandatory.

He should have re-bloody-scheduled.

Behind her, Anna walked in, mug in hand. 'Here you go.'

'Thanks.' She took it and breathed it in, waiting for the usual comforting magic to hit.

Yeah, right, like coffee's going to do it.

Only one thing was going to make her feel better...

'Can I get you anything else?'

The man's head on a plate?

'Could you ask Mr Wright to join me?'

'Sure.' Anna turned to leave and paused to look back over her shoulder. 'Would you like me to do it right now?'

She set her coffee down and nodded with a smile.

Her PA returned it, a mirroring spark in her eye. 'No problem.'

She waited for Anna to close the door and then lowered herself into her chair, smoothing her hands over her black pencil skirt. She took out her laptop and placed it on the desk, interlacing her fingers and resting them on top as she waited.

It didn't take long. There was a short rap on the door and she forced her shoulders to relax. 'Come in.'

'Jennifer,' he greeted, entering the room and closing the door behind him.

The thrill of his proximity mixed with her wrath and it was a wonder she could raise her eyes to his, avoiding the open collar of his shirt, the appealing frame within the designer suit, the hint of his cologne crossing the distance between them.

She swallowed subtly, praying he wouldn't spy it, and forced words out in a level voice. 'Marcus, please take a seat.'

His eyes flickered. 'You know I'm in the middle of a meeting, right?'

'One that I was supposed to attend—yes.'

He wavered. 'We're just about to wrap it up with a vote—why don't you come and join us?'

'A vote?' She raised her brows with a wry smile. 'On something I have yet to be brought up to speed with?'

He tucked his jacket behind his arms and slipped his hands into his pockets. She didn't want to think about how the move pulled his shirt taut against his firm expanse of chest.

'Well, I would hope that you'd have enough faith in Maxine to trust her opinion—she's quite impressive.'

Something smarted but she ignored it. 'Please take a seat, Marcus.'

She needed him sitting, with at least some of him concealed by furnishings.

He cleared his throat and walked towards the chair across from her, his eyes flicking over her, their chocolate depths assessing.

'I don't have long,' he said, placing his hands on the arms of the chair and resting back into it.

He gave the impression of being relaxed but his eyes were sharp, doing their damnedest to read her.

She'd save him the trouble.

Turning in her seat, she got to her feet and stepped around her desk, feeling his eyes follow her. She didn't stop until she came alongside him, resting back against the desk-edge so that she towered over him.

Much better.

He looked up, his gaze sweeping her front, and for

a split second she saw it, the unguarded fierce hunger, and it almost broke through her anger. *Almost*.

'I trust Maxine implicitly,' she began, 'but that's not the issue here.'

'Mind telling me what is?'

His deep husky voice reverberated through her belly. His nearness was taking over that part of her she wanted to ignore.

'The fact you need me to explain worries me.'

'If this is about me holding a meeting without you, then I'm afraid there was no choice in that.'

'There's *always* a choice.'

She crossed her arms over her middle and saw his eyes fall briefly as the air-conditioned draught swept through the expanding V of her blue silk blouse. He might not believe in mixing business and pleasure, but his body certainly did.

Power rushed through her, upping her resolve as she asked, 'How can you hold a meeting to discuss the future of our product development without me?'

He shifted in his seat, his hands coming up to clasp one another upon his lap, over his… She smiled inwardly.

'It's complicated, and I need to get back in there to get this wrapped up,' he said. 'I have a conference call shortly with the States.'

'Okay, then, give me a high-level summary.'

He rolled his head on his shoulders, his tension evident. 'It's been brought to my attention that one of our competitors is about to go live with a product Tech-Incorp should have delivered first. We need to throw everything at it so we beat them to it.'

'And you couldn't wait until this afternoon to have your meeting?'

'No. I want this dealt with before my call with the States and I want a press release drafted ASAP.'

'My question remains—could it not have waited?'

'Look, my head of marketing over there has been trying to reach me since seven last night—that's how urgent this is. And had we not been—'

He broke off and a rising tide of anger within her had the word *'fucking'* bursting from her lips.

His eyes flashed, a muscle moving in his jaw. 'Yes.'

'Then you wouldn't have missed it?'

'No.'

The atmosphere shifted. Memories of them entwined, of the passion that had seemed impossible to sate, were making the air practically crackle between them.

'I need to get back in there.'

The raw edge to his voice, his obvious discomfort, made her want to push him that little bit more, and so, outwardly casual, she crossed one stocking-clad thigh over the other. His eyes traced the movement, just as she'd known they would.

'Fair enough,' she said, 'but let this be a warning. If you treat me like a subordinate again, then this "relationship"…' she gestured between them, the nail of one finger trailing down his front before returning to her own '…you and me, will get a whole lot more inconvenient than you first pitched it to be.'

His eyes blazed, his tongue brushing across his lower lip, and suddenly her own tongue felt too thick for her throat.

'I know what I said, Jennifer.'

He shifted, one hand curving around her hip, and her skin buzzed uncontrollably beneath his touch. *Don't react, don't react...*

'And I stand by it. It wasn't the best start to our working relationship.'

She raised her chin and looked down at him, doing her damnedest to maintain her composure. But words weren't forthcoming—not through the drunken haze of his touch.

'What I should have added is that I don't regret it one bit.'

Her breath caught at his honesty.

Did she regret it? If she was honest, did she wish they'd never gone there?

His thumb started to circle over her, the skin beneath treated to a whirlpool of sensation, and her body answered with a resounding *no*.

'And what I should also like to make very clear to you,' he said darkly, rising to his feet and side-stepping to stand before her, his proximity keeping her pressed into the desk, 'is that you should never tease me—not unless you're willing to deal with the consequences.'

She sensed his other hand come up, felt his fingers brushing against her jaw, sending a traitorous shiver down her spine.

'You assured me you would behave,' she blurted suddenly.

Christ, did she have to sound so breathless? So desperate?

He didn't budge, didn't even blink, and she tried again. 'You have your rules too.'

'That's the funny thing about rules.' He smiled

mercilessly, his eyes fixed on her parted lips. 'They're all the more fun when they get broken.'

He dipped his head slowly. Alarm bells rang through her head. *Knee him in the balls, push him away—anything!*

Instead she whimpered, the sound erupting from nowhere. And watched with self-loathing as his smile became one of victory and he stepped back. An immediate chill swept down her front.

'Like I said, you're welcome to join us,' he said, his palms turned outwards in an overly innocent gesture, 'but it's time I got back in there.'

And then he turned and went, opening and closing the door behind him, his message clear. He didn't expect her to follow.

Well, fuck that.

She breathed through the daze—the desire, the frustration, the anger…

What the hell had possessed her?

She knew, all right. She'd been playing with fire; wanting to replace the shitty feeling of being undermined by overpowering him, and she'd used her sexuality to do it. It had been a low move. It was beneath her.

But the rush—the way it had made her feel—beat any boardroom conquest. That was until he'd turned the tables on her.

She took a far more controlled breath, pushing herself up off the desk. It was time to show him that she didn't need her sexuality to do that. It was time to show him that, professionally, she was someone he didn't want to screw over.

Screw with, *on the other hand…*

Quit it!

She drowned the thought in some coffee and focused on her laptop.

She'd show him.

'Apologies.'

His eyes shot to the doorway, to the exquisite redhead holding her laptop over her chest, coffee in hand.

Fuck.

Marcus wasn't ready to have her in the same room again—not yet. He'd expected her to stay away, prayed that she would.

She was stronger than he'd given her credit for. He shouldn't really be surprised. Not when she had surprised him on every other score.

'I had some urgent business that needed attending to,' she continued, addressing the room, her smooth, honeyed tone washing over him, hinting at the husky resonance it gained when she came apart under his hand, his mouth...

She walked towards them, her expression pointed as she looked at him.

Introductions, you idiot!

He cleared his throat. 'Jennifer, this is Gary, my Head of Product Development, and his close second, Dan.'

The two men stood as she placed her coffee at the table they occupied and her hand reached out to shake each of theirs in turn. Her smile was that soul-crushingly gorgeous one that had his brain departing. And probably his team's now too.

For fuck's sake, stick to work. Not a day in and

you've almost thrown your assurances out of the window. So much for keeping yourself in bloody check…

But then, she'd been the one to push first, the one to put—

'Marcus?'

They all looked at him expectantly, especially Jennifer, who'd been the one to say his name, her brow raised as she said it.

'Care to fill me in on where you're at?'

The spark to her eyes said she knew *exactly* where his head was at, and it wasn't at work.

This just kept getting better and better.

He gave a brisk nod, forcing himself to get with it. 'Maxine was just summing up the impact of my proposal on your product stream.'

Her eyes narrowed. 'I assume we're talking about using some of our resources to get Tech-Incorp's product out of the door ahead of schedule?'

She'd hit the nail on the head and, to her credit, there had been no emotion in her supposition.

'That's right,' Maxine said, stepping forward to give Jennifer a copy of the project plans she'd scribbled her amendments on. 'The impact shouldn't be too great, but it will mean pushing back on Projects Azure and Topaz.'

Jennifer nodded, placing her laptop and the papers upon the table, her eyes scanning the pages. 'Do you have time to give me a brief breakdown of this Tech-Incorp product?'

She looked to Marcus and he immediately looked to Gary. 'Do the honours?'

'Sure.'

That was him out of her sight for a spell. He settled back into the chair behind his desk, letting Jennifer join the others at the table while Gary sold the product to the room.

He could see Jennifer liked it. But if he'd thought her eyes being off him would reduce her hold over him, he'd been wrong. Watching her unhindered had just given him an added opportunity to appreciate her further—the professional Jennifer, asking the right questions, listening carefully and offering her own insightful input. And all in a beautifully captivating package.

Could she be any more perfect?

'I assume Maxine has told you we have something similar in development?' She directed the question to them all, pulling Marcus back to the conversation at hand.

Maxine nodded. 'I have.'

'And I assume you have debated which product should get the weight of the combined team behind it?'

'We have.'

It was Gary who gave the confirmation, but Jennifer looked to Maxine, wanting her affirmation.

'We have,' she said tentatively, her gaze flitting over the other attendees as a hint of colour crept into her cheeks. 'And I did suggest we incorporate some of our features.'

'But we decided that would take too long,' Dan argued.

Jennifer pinned him with a look. 'What kind of timescales are we talking?'

'A few weeks,' Marcus confirmed over Dan's reply. 'At least I'm hoping so. My conference call this afternoon will confirm it.'

'Then I think we should put time into ensuring the product is the best it can be, in the timescale permitted, and if that means merging specifications then so be it.'

'But we're practically at the finish line,' Gary pitched in.

'I understand that.' She gave him a killer smile, but her eyes were hard. 'Nonetheless, my team has worked hard on this product to date, and for you to sweep in now so soon after your arrival in this firm and have it canned would be unwise.'

The room fell silent as the impact of her words hit home.

'Not only will this ensure our employees don't feel shafted by your presence,' she continued, 'we can also ensure we put the best product out there.'

Marcus felt both men look to him, sensed Maxine's smile of approval, but his eyes were locked with hers and he was lost in them, his admiration swelling with irritating vigour.

'Very well,' he heard himself say. 'Get the teams together. They have until the end of the week to get it mapped out and underway.'

Her lips quirked with triumph and, *fuck*, did he want to obliterate it with his own.

'Seems to me you have a lot to get done.' He glanced over them all, settling on Jennifer last. 'Why don't you get to it?'

They all stood, save for her.

'I assume you'd like to stay for this conference call?' he said.

She gave him a brisk nod, the movement drawing his eye to the crystal droplets swinging from each ear and to the soft, expanse of skin just behind. His mouth dried. The desire to taste her was instinctive— to drive out the whimper he so loved to hear, to trail a path from there all the way to her collarbone and further still…

The room had emptied before he came to, and he did so with force. 'Are you doing battle with *me*? Or are you truly fighting the corner for your product and your team?'

She gave him a coy smile, crossing her legs as she brushed a distracting hand across her thigh.

'I *want* to say I'm being entirely noble…'

She cocked her head serenely, her eyes dancing with mischief, and God help him the rush beneath his waist was instant.

'But doing battle with you is kind of fun.'

'Did you not listen to my warning?'

'Oh, I listened,' she said smoothly.

His mouth opened to respond but nothing came— nothing that would make sense.

What did he want to propose? Did he really want to act on his threat? And where would that leave him? Leave them?

He was rescued by the phone ringing, signalling his incoming US call.

She rose from her seat to join him at his desk and he answered the call.

He'd have liked to say his attention moved fully to the call. He'd have also liked to say that for the remainder of that week his focus revolved fully around work.

But he hadn't been born a liar.

He wasn't about to start being one now.

As for his assurance that he would keep himself in check—it was crippling him. Her constant presence was a permanent tease that no one could see off. Or rather, no woman.

And his mood suffered with it.

Celibacy, it turned out, was *not* good for him—on any level.

CHAPTER ELEVEN

SHE'D BEEN READING the same article for the last hour and still it wouldn't compute.

What an utter waste of an early start.

'You can't go on like this,' she muttered under her breath, taking up her coffee mug and rising out of her swivel chair to head to the window.

She looked down at the street below, at the early-morning commuters going about their business.

Were any of them suffering the same way? Their thoughts stuck where they shouldn't be, on something else, on someone else?

There'd been a closeness between them that night, when they'd opened up about their pasts. A closeness she'd never shared with anyone outside of her family. She doubted he had either. She'd sensed his disclosure had come from him feeling he owed it to her, that he'd had to force back his unease at doing so. And all that he'd told her of what he'd been through. Her heart swelled anew. To have pushed through it when many others might have let it ruin them...

But then wasn't he ruined in some way? Broken, almost? She'd seen the hurt he harboured, the bitterness, the discomfort when he'd talked of his grand-

ready to give notice. And she's worked for him for five years.'

'Maybe he's finding it hard to get his feet under the table here.'

'If that's the case, maybe you could help him?'

Anna's smile was innocent, unlike Jennifer's brain, which was delighting in the many ways she could help settle him. None of which were acceptable.

'If he carries on like this he's going to become a thorn in your side too—albeit a good-looking thorn. But still, you don't need the stress.'

Anna was right. She didn't. And maybe she should be more concerned. If the two of them were struggling to function, how on earth was the business supposed to?

'I'll speak to him when he gets in.' She glanced at her watch. It was late for him, and the worry Anna had triggered started to spread.

'Speak of the devil,' her PA said, looking to the outer office beyond the glass and the man now striding through it.

No fucking way.

'It should be forbidden for any man to come in looking like that.'

Jennifer barely registered her PA's words, her mouth parting, the hand holding her coffee lowering as her eyes followed him across the office. He'd been for a run—likely a long and punishing one, judging by his slick body, his clothing clinging to every honed muscle, making her fingers tingle with their first-hand knowledge of it.

She swallowed and moved to tear her eyes away before he could catch her gawping—but too late.

His energised gaze swept to hers, his smile not quite reaching his eyes as he acknowledged her.

She tried for a smile too. *Hell, hers was probably just as off.*

'Well, there's no time like the present,' Anna said, seemingly oblivious as she made for the door. 'I'll tell him you need a word, shall I?'

'No.'

Anna looked back at her, eyes narrowed, and, taking a breath, she expanded with reasoned logic. 'I mean, yes, but I'm sure he'd like a shower first.'

'I guess,' said Anna, glancing back at him wistfully. 'Still, I'll just let him know you'll be needing him when he's ready.'

And with that she was gone, returning not a minute later, face aglow. 'He says to call by in ten.'

'Okay.'

Did he say he'd be appropriately attired by then? she wanted to ask, but didn't dare. It wouldn't do to give Anna the impression she was overly bothered.

But it was bad enough that she already knew first-hand the consequences of catching him post-workout— or mid-workout, or whatever he'd been that day in his apartment. She didn't need a repeat.

Ten minutes—she'd give him fifteen, just to be sure.

He checked his watch. She should be here by now. He glanced to the doorway, across the quiet office through the glass. No sign. Should he just go to her?

But maybe she'd got caught up in something. He didn't want to appear eager. Hell, his biggest challenge in the role to date had been to strike the right balance in his dealings with her, to dampen his relentless need to see her. Hunting her down didn't fit with that.

But she'd asked to see him—she'd given him a reason...

Christ, stop overthinking everything!

His run to work that morning had been about trying to clear his mind, to get himself focused, back to how he'd been before she'd come into his life. What it had really proved was that it couldn't be done. Not easily. The only way he could foresee being able to think straight by day was having her in his bed by night. And surely that was madness.

But, madness or not, he was fast running out of options.

Maybe she was too. Maybe that was why she wanted to see him. *Hell, he could hope.*

Grabbing his mobile, he made for the door just as the device started ringing in his palm. He checked the screen and halted in his tracks—*Gran.*

He cut the call instinctively. He'd text her back... tell her he was busy and that he'd—

It started to ring again and he thrust his fingers through his hair. The early hour, the repeated ringing—it had to be urgent. In spite of his recent run, ice ran through his veins and he glanced up, spying movement across the office. Jennifer was approaching and still his phone rang.

He looked from it, to her, and back again, knowing what he had to do and fearing it all the same.

Just tell her you'll call her back.

Jennifer rapped on his door and he gestured for her to enter as he swiped the screen to answer the call, raising the phone to his ear. 'Hey, Gran—can I call you back in just a minute?'

'It's me, son.'

The familiar voice of his grandfather rasped down the line and he frowned in confusion. 'Pops?'

'Sorry to call you so early, but it's your grand-mother. She's in hospital.'

The world around him closed in. His lungs sucked in air. 'Hospital?'

'They suspect she's suffered a stroke.' His grand-father cleared his throat, the sound clearly a cover for the crack in his voice, and Marcus's own chest tightened further, his grip around the phone tighten-ing with it.

'How bad is it?'

'She's stable,' his grandfather said. 'They say she's doing well. She's resting now, but... Well, I just thought you'd like to know.'

Guilt wrapped around him, suffocating him. He looked to Jennifer. Her concern was shining bright in her furrowed gaze, her arms wrapped defensively around her middle.

'Of course,' he heard himself say. 'Will you keep me posted?'

'Absolutely, son. I'll let you get back to it.'

He felt lost. He didn't know how to react, what to say. All he knew was that he hated the feeling work-ing its way through his gut.

'Marcus, are you still there?

'Sorry, Pops. I'll call you later?'

'Sure.'

He sensed his grandfather hanging up and the one thing he knew he had to say sprang forward. 'Pops?'

'Yes, son?'

'Give her my love.'

He heard him sigh down the line. 'Of course.'

And then he was gone.

'What's happened?' Jennifer asked, stepping forward, one hand reaching out to rest on his arm.

He stepped back instantly, breaking the contact, something like panic hitting him. The concern in her voice, the softness in her touch, was a soothing balm to the raging torrent within.

How could she do that so effortlessly?

His skin prickled, the chill intensifying as worry for his Gran heightened.

'Marcus?' She frowned up at him, arms returning to hug her middle. 'What is it?'

'It's my grandmother.' He walked away from her, eyes averted as he headed to his desk. 'She's in hospital. They suspect she's suffered a stroke.'

She made a small sound, but he refused to look her way, speaking before she had the chance to. 'What did you need to see me for?'

'Marcus,' she said softly, 'look at me.'

Christ, couldn't she take the hint?

He didn't want to talk about it. Not with her. Not with anyone.

He shut his face down and forced his eyes to do her bidding. 'I don't want to talk about it.'

She studied him, the bright office lights glinting in her compassion-filled gaze. 'Okay, but don't you think you should be leaving?'

'Leaving?' He frowned at her. 'Are you mad? We have a product meeting in under an hour.'

She mimicked his frown. 'And the woman who practically raised you is lying in a hospital bed!'

'Apparently she's stable…she's doing well.' He threw his grandfather's reassurances at her, purposefully ignoring the tug of her words. 'She doesn't need me there.'

'Of course she needs you there.' She stepped towards him, stopping as he backed up again. 'You should go.'

Go. Go back. To Wales.

His stomach clenched and he shook his head at her, turning away once more. *What could she know of it? She'd never understand.*

'Did you need me urgently, or can it wait until later?' he asked.

'Marcus, for what it's worth, time is precious,' she said. 'I'd give anything to have had more with my father. Like I'm sure you would with your mum.'

He clamped his eyes shut, grateful she couldn't see the effect her words were having.

'Don't let this…whatever it is…get in the way of the time you have left with your grandparents.'

She went quiet, the room with it. And he refused to turn, to move, any response impossible.

Eventually she sighed, and the sound of her heels clipping against the tiled floor told him she was leaving. Relief mingled with an irrational surge of disappointment.

'Please,' he heard her say as the door swung open, 'just think about it. I can hold the fort here.'

And then she was gone, the door clicking shut, her heels receding on the other side.

Above the churning a warmth started to spread—

admiration, respect, something more…? *Damned if he knew.* Her concern for him, for his situation, flummoxed him. The sensation swelled with freakish intent and confusion paralysed him to the spot.

What the hell did he do with any of it?

CHAPTER TWELVE

CONCENTRATE, JENNIFER. It's none of your business. It's not your concern...

The document on the screen before her swirled grey over white, not making sense. It had been the same for most of the day—as if she was in some weird state of limbo, swinging from the need to go to him and demand that he leave to wanting to maintain her professional distance and keeping well out of it.

She'd already overstepped. She knew it. But she hadn't been able to help herself. Not when she'd seen the distress in every line of his beautiful face. And her worry had only mounted when he had not left. Not only that, he'd barely spoken to her—barely even looked at her since.

She felt crushed. The terrifying realisation had hit home that she cared far too much—that against her better judgement and her best-laid plans for the future he'd got under her skin. When she'd looked into his eyes and seen the desolation, the fear and the confusion, she'd wanted desperately to go to him, to soothe it away. But he'd made it clear he wanted none of that from her. In fact, he couldn't have moved away faster or dismissed her any more decisively.

She should be grateful for the reminder of where their professional line lay. But it wasn't gratitude making her gut ache and her mind wander…

She pressed a hand to her tummy, closing her eyes slowly and opening them on the computer screen, refocusing her efforts.

There were things she had to get done…things that were her responsibility.

A sharp rap on the door had her jumping and she looked up to the glass as Anna swung it open. 'Sorry, I didn't mean to startle you, but have you seen the time?'

She stilled, her eyes snapping to the clock on her screen. *Shit*—she had forty-five minutes until her train to Leeds departed.

How could she have lost sight of that?

She shot up.

What a damn stupid question.

She started shoving things into her bag, her mind racing with what she needed to take.

'Sorry—I would've come sooner, only I've been wrestling with that bloody photocopier again.'

'It's not your fault. I might just—'

'What's the hurry?'

In her panic she hadn't seen Marcus approach, hadn't even sensed it, and now he was in the same room with no forewarning and she struggled to breathe.

'Jennifer's late for her train to Leeds,' Anna supplied.

She plucked her loaded bag off the desk and headed straight for them, eyes averted and grabbing her coat off the stand as she went. 'I have to get home to my family.'

They parted for her to pass, but she could feel him move, hot on her tail.

'Colin will get you to the station.'

She paused, turning to argue.

Don't be an idiot—not when he's the best chance you have.

'Thank you.'

He was already activating his mobile and she looked to Anna—anything to ease his pull and the painful ache that now accompanied it.

'Do you have those info packs for me?'

'Sure.'

She headed to her desk and gathered them up while Marcus issued his driver with instructions and hung up.

'I'll join you in the car,' he said to her. 'There's something we need to discuss.'

Her lips parted with another impulsive refusal but Anna's return silenced her.

'Here you go.' She passed her the documentation. 'They have Lucy's approval.'

'Thank you.' She slotted them into her bag and managed a farewell smile. 'Have a good weekend.'

'You too.'

She watched her PA turn and walk away, her nerves rocketing as she was left with Marcus. Pretty much just the two of them in the open office, most of the staff having escaped for after-work drinks to ring in the weekend. But they might as well have been in a broom cupboard for the effect his nearness was having on her.

'He's ready for us,' he said, urging her to the lift.

She took in his black shirt, sleeves rolled back, collar open, and self-preservation took charge. 'Do you want to get a jacket first?'

'I'm good.'

She met his darkened gaze and tripped out.

This is madness. Make your own way...miss the train...get another—anything but... Christ, did he want to talk privately to tell her she'd overstepped?

Heat flooded her cheeks.

God, no, she knew that well enough already. She didn't—

His hand curved around her elbow and her head emptied, her body being propelled forth under his encouragement.

Outside, Colin stood, rear door of the car open and at the ready. He'd got his instructions well enough, and no sooner were they inside than he was in the front and pulling out into traffic.

'You didn't need to do this,' she said, her sights fixed on the outside world speeding past, her hands gripped together on her lap.

'I wanted the opportunity to apologise.'

Surprise had her eyes sweeping to his. 'What for?'

'This morning. I was short with you.'

He shook his head, the movement sending a lock of hair across his forehead and drawing her eye to the crazy state of the remainder. A sign of much hand-thrusting that day, she was sure.

Sadness consumed her. *He should've gone.*

She looked away before he could read her. 'It wasn't my place to get involved. I shouldn't have interfered.'

'Be that as it may, you were right.'

Her chest tightened, her throat with it, and she straightened her spine. 'I was?'

'Yes.'

He reached out to brush some escaped hair behind her ear and her breath caught. A red-hot shiver ran to her core, a warmth taking up camp there that she was powerless to prevent.

'I didn't like hearing it but, yes, you were right. I need to go.'

'Then why are you still here?' she asked, relief at his decision drowned out by the over-familiarity of his touch.

Don't soften. It's good that he's going but it doesn't change who he is to you. Who you are to him. Business partners. No more.

'Why delay by taking me to the station?'

'Because you need to make your train and I needed to apologise. Don't worry—I'm leaving straight after. My grandparents already know I'm coming.' His eyes turned inward momentarily as a smile played about his lips. 'It felt good to tell them. And I have you to thank for that.'

He studied her, eyes unwavering. The air was charged with an unidentifiable emotion and she struggled to say, 'I'm glad.'

'Me too,' he said softly. 'I would have left earlier but there were things I needed to take care of—and then there was you. I couldn't go without apologising. And, though I hate to admit it, building up the nerve has taken some doing.'

'Chicken?' The realisation ripped through the heavy mood, making her feel strangely light-headed.

He grinned *that* grin. 'Something like that. I'm not one for admitting I was wrong.'

She returned his smile, his honesty making it impossible not to. 'Fair enough.'

'But there's something else I need to discuss before I disappear off.'

Her skin prickled, her smile becoming forced, 'Something else?'

He nodded, and the deepening sincerity in his gaze held her captive as he reached out.

'The truth is, I've not been myself all week because of you.'

His fingers brushed the nape of her neck and the red-hot shiver sparked anew, multiplying fiercely.

'Trying to act like nothing happened between us has been torture. Knowing you're there, just down the corridor, and I can't have you—it's all I can think about.'

She clutched her hands in her lap, unable to look away, unable to move, the fear of what she might do holding her still as the warmth in the pit of her belly became a rolling ache.

'I can't work,' he continued. 'I can't sleep. I can't go home without the memory of you being there plaguing me, teasing me...'

His honesty pushed through her defences, toying with her heartstrings, teasing her with a multitude of possibilities that no amount of trepidation could quell.

'The truth is...' he repeated, and her every sense waited for what he would confess next, a spark of hope flaring that had no right to exist. 'I don't think I can function properly without having you, without letting this thing between us take its course.'

She frowned, a real chill working its way in.

Take its course? Did he think it was finite? That he would wake up one morning and it would be gone—the want, the need, the persistent ache?

Isn't that what you thought? When you asked for that extra night, didn't you hope it would do the same?

Hell, she knew better now.

It wasn't that simple.

Not for her.

She took hold of his fingers, forcing herself to stop his heady caress. 'Please don't, Marcus.'

She sounded weak, but her hand lifted his away and she returned her own to her lap, her eyes to the window.

'Don't tell me you don't feel it too,' he pushed. 'Don't tell me you haven't struggled all week. I know you've tried to avoid me. I've seen how you escape the office. I've seen how you look my way when you think people aren't looking.'

She swallowed, shaking her head in denial.

'And these,' he said, gently flicking the crystal droplet hanging from the ear that was closest to him, 'are killing me.'

What?

She looked to him, brow furrowed. 'Why?'

'The way they swing when you move your head, like they did just then… You do it in meetings and I'm sucked right in, drawn to the skin just *here*.' He swirled the pad of his thumb over the exact spot. 'Remembering how it feels, how it tastes, how it makes you whimper…'

Christ, she wanted to whimper right now—could feel the need bursting through her.

Don't do it.

'You know what else it makes me want to do?'

She felt her head shake and he leant in, his breath sweeping over her sensitised neck and making her tremble with want even as her brain screamed *Stop him!*

'It makes me want to drive that sound out of you… that small, tiny noise that starts just here,' he whispered, his mouth devouring the space his fingers had just occupied.

Her body exploded in a rush, that whimper breaking free, the impulsive sound jarring out as a feeble, 'Don't…'

'Why?' he rasped with need, cajoling her along despite everything else telling her otherwise. 'Why deny something that feels so right?'

'Because it's bad for business.'

'Denying it is bad for business.'

His tongue did a crazy dance over her skin, prickling over the area with dizzying effect.

'Or are you telling me your week has been particularly fruitful?'

As he said the words he curved his hand around her neck on the other side, coaxing her to arch her neck and grant him greater access.

'Christ, Marcus, I'm trying to save us from potential disaster.'

She was trying to save herself from a broken heart.

'I admire your diligence,' he whispered against her dampened skin, 'but you're worth the risk.'

Why did that feel so special? Why had her tummy gone to goo?

Something broke inside her—something that drove

her hands into his hair and turned her body to liquid beneath him. It was the need to have him fill her, complete her, take away the painful ache, the worrying thoughts…

'You taste like honey and vanilla,' he breathed against her, his fingers following the arch of her neck, stroking across the curve of her collarbone and dipping to meet with the fastened buttons of her blouse.

And then his fingers were undoing, and she couldn't stop him—didn't want to. The throb between her legs was desperate, her breathing erratic, her nails biting into his scalp.

He parted the fabric, letting the cool air of the car sweep across her front, and he cursed under his breath. 'I can't get enough of this.'

She looked to him through the haze, saw his gaze burning into her skin and she hit insanity, the lust curling through her obliterating all reason.

'I need to taste you.'

His voice was raw, his face asking for permission and, Christ, she couldn't speak, could only nod.

'We don't have long.'

It seemed he was making excuses, but for what she couldn't understand—until he dropped to his knees and pushed her skirt to her thighs.

'I'd devour every last bit of you if we had the time, but as it is…'

Cupping her behind, he pulled her forward and shoved her legs apart, pressing her knees back against the cold leather. Somewhere in the rational part of her brain she knew she wanted to fight him, and knew why, but the painful reasoning, the painful ache—she wanted it all gone.

Obliterated by him.

'Hold yourself open for me.' He drew her hands in to replace his own, coaxing her to obey. 'That's it…'

He rested back, his eyes drinking her in, his burning desire choking the very air from her lungs, and then he reached out, hooking his fingers into her lace panties and pulling them aside, his free hand coming up to spread her open before him.

'So wet…so fucking beautiful,' he murmured, his head dropping forward, his mouth honing in on its target.

Fuck!

She threw her head back into the leather, a spasm shooting through her as he took her clit in his teeth. Pleasure ripped through her, and her nails bit into the skin of her inner thighs as she held herself open.

He worked her, his mouth sucking, tongue flicking, teeth nipping. And then his fingers thrust into her, invading her like his cock would. One, two—*yes, fuck, yes*—three, four—*Christ, yes*. She ground herself against him wildly. She couldn't fit more… she couldn't—and then he curved in his thumb, his whole hand fucking her deep as his tongue lashed over her clit.

'Come for me, baby,' he urged.

And the heat in his voice, the endearment rumbling over her, his fist completing her—she was gone. Shattering over him, screaming his name as her whole world fell apart around her.

He sipped at her, withdrawing his fingers slowly and holding her hooded gaze as he licked them clean. 'I don't think I could ever tire of tasting you.'

If only that were true, came her internal voice,

louder now in the aftermath, and she felt chilled, snapping her eyes away.

'We shouldn't have done that.'

The bitterness, the self-loathing was back. It bit into her tone and he shifted into the seat alongside her, his confusion penetrating the air.

'Are you telling me you didn't like it?'

He smoothed his hand over her thigh and she pulled her skirt back into position, brushing him away. Moving to fasten her blouse next, she felt the need to cry, sudden and chilling.

'We can't work together and do this.'

'I beg to differ,' he said confidently. 'I think this is essential if we are going to get our heads back in the game once more.'

She shook her head.

Back in the game? Was that all this was to him?

'Hear me out,' he said. 'We both work too hard to support any decent relationship outside of work.'

She didn't respond, her fingers shaking as they fastened up the last button.

'So why not get this fix on the doorstep?'

She could feel the heat of his gaze on her as her brain struggled with the very idea he was putting forward, as her body impulsively demanded her agreement.

'We're both grown-ups,' he pressed. 'We can sate this need, free our brains to concentrate on work and not worry about the usual relationship baggage.'

No baggage. No feelings. Just sex.

Jennifer felt her heart shrivel and hated it for being so pathetic. Why couldn't she simply say yes? No one had ever driven her as wild as he could. She'd never desired anyone the way she desired him.

But you've never been as crazy about someone either.

'Take the weekend,' he said into her continued silence. 'Think about it and you can give me your answer on Monday.'

How did he remain so focused when her entire world was shattering?

Because he wants this, wants you... But he doesn't want more.

That was the real issue. He could take the sex and leave the rest.

She only wished she was capable of the same.

'I'll think about it,' she said, grateful that the car was pulling up at the station and she'd soon be free.

Shrugging on her jacket, she didn't wait for Colin. As soon as the car stopped she opened the door and stepped out, closing it behind her. She didn't say goodbye, she didn't thank his driver—she needed space, *now.*

It turned out space wasn't enough.

He hounded her the entire journey home.

She threw herself into her to-do list: co-ordinating Tony's rehab, paying the bills, managing her inbox and so on. But he was always there...at the back of her mind.

By the time the taxi pulled up outside her home her head was swimming and the tension knotting at the base of her neck signalled the onset of a full-blown migraine. She rubbed at it as she stepped out of the car and followed the driver to the boot.

'Jenny!'

She turned to see Kate bounding down the stone-stepped entrance towards her. 'Hey, sis!' she called, turning back to the driver as he handed over her weekend bag. 'Thank you.'

'You're welcome, miss.'

Kate's arms came around her from behind, squeezing her tight. 'It's so good to see you.'

'You too.' She turned, easing her sister's embrace enough to give her a kiss on the cheek and hook her arm through hers. 'How's Mum?'

'She's good—really good,' Kate said emphatically as they headed towards the house. 'She's reading in the library—we've found it helps settle her with the nights drawing in.'

Jennifer nodded. It was good that they'd found something to help with the evenings.

'Tell you what—give me your stuff and I'll dump it in your room. You go and see Mum.'

'Great,' she said, even as she felt the familiar pull of anxiety bed in.

Kate took her bags and bounded back into the house. Jennifer followed slowly, her belly twisting with nerves as she crossed over the threshold and headed down the hall that led to the library. The smell of food reached her. Marie, their housekeeper, was likely making her favourite—lasagne. But hunger was the last thing on her mind.

She paused at the library door, her hand resting on the handle, and took a breath, her shoulders rolling back as she braced herself for whatever was to come.

She opened the door and stepped inside. The room was well lit, the fire notably out. Her mother sat reading in her favourite chair overlooking the grounds, although the curtains were now drawn against the darkening outdoors.

'Mum?' she said tentatively.

Her mother looked up, lowering the book into her lap as she dipped her reading glasses to look at her.

A smile of recognition spread across her face. 'Jennifer, darling, you're home.'

The air left her lungs in a whoosh. Her mum knew who she was today. *Fuck you, Alzheimer's!*

She swept across the room to draw her into a bear hug, emotion welling as she held her mum close.

'Why, Jennifer, you're going to suffocate me if you keep this up.'

'Sorry, Mum.' She backed off a little, her eyes raking over her mother's face, taking in her glowing complexion and bright green eyes with glee. 'I've missed you.'

Marcus had made the decision to drive himself to Wales, keen to have the distraction of the roads to occupy him. And the solitude. He didn't like the way he'd been all week and he certainly didn't like the way he was now.

He'd watched her enter the station with the feeling that he'd just made an epic mistake swelling uncomfortably in his gut.

But it didn't make sense. She wanted him. He wanted her. It was win-win. Only her face, the way her post-orgasm glow had drained so swiftly, had twisted him up inside.

Had he gone too far? Did she truly think he was endangering their business? Was that what it all came down to?

He couldn't believe it. It didn't sit right.

The sign for his home town lit up in his headlights, blurred through the rain, and his heart skipped, his stomach lurched and his thoughts quit, drowned out by the memories that came pouring in uninvited.

He shifted in his seat, squinting through the windscreen to take in the surroundings that never seemed to change: the stone-built terraced houses lining the road, the corner shop that wasn't on a corner, his primary school—the gates of which he'd stood at many a night, waiting for his father to collect him and eventually setting off alone, scared witless in the dark.

His grip over the steering wheel tightened and he diverted his gaze straight ahead. He'd left that life behind long ago…and neglected his grandparents in doing so.

His throat closed over and he swallowed through it.

He was back now. That was what mattered.

He stopped at a set of lights, the only sound that of his windscreen wipers beating away the rain, and then a laugh reached him—the high-pitched ripple of a teen. He turned his head towards it. A young couple were just leaving a house, a lad with his arm hooked around his girl, his grin happy, her laugh even more so.

The scene reached inside the car, engulfing him with its warmth, coaxing out a smile as his hold over the wheel eased.

Just because it had been bad for him, it didn't make it bad for everyone. It had never been the place that had been the problem…

And yet he'd kept fleeing it, when all he'd ever

wanted was to flee *him*. But he wasn't his father, and his father was long gone.

His eyes pricked at the sudden lightness inside him

Before him, the lights turned green, but he didn't move. He was caught up in a conversation with her—with Jennifer. Remembering her words, her compassion.

'Don't let this get in the way of what time you have left.'

The strange warmth from that morning spread like wildfire. *How had she done it?* Gone through the death of her father and ploughed it into something so wonderful—a successful business, a stable future for her family.

She didn't run from the darkness or live in fear of the *what if*.

Not like him. Fear and darkness had been his driving force since for ever.

A horn honked behind him and he flashed his lights apologetically, setting the car in motion.

Could he change? And what did change even mean? Would it make him happy? Was happiness even possible for him?

Contentment, yes...

But happiness ?

CHAPTER THIRTEEN

JENNIFER RACED BACK through the grounds, her breath sending puffs of white into the crisp morning air.

She loved it here. The fields, the open spaces, the wildlife. Even in autumn, with the leaves disappearing from the trees and the flowers dying back, there was still a serenity to it all, especially when the sky was as blue as it was today.

It was the perfect day for a run, the perfect opportunity to forget everything for a while and just enjoy the peace and fresh air. Only her thoughts had been far from peaceful, wrapped up as they were in a certain male and his far too appealing proposition.

Not even the fear of falling too deep could stop her thinking on it.

It had kept her up until the early hours and sent her out running at the crack of dawn. Anything to kill the restlessness it instilled.

But the run hadn't worked. She was back, slightly less agitated but no less distracted. Frustrated, she yanked at the laces of her trainers and slipped them off. Picking them up to pad through the old trades-man's entrance and into the kitchen, she felt the cold stone floor biting through her socks, the sensation soothing her with its familiarity.

She entered the kitchen and set a fresh pot of coffee going before grabbing some cold water from the fridge. She had drunk most of it when Kate walked in.

'I hope you've put enough on for me.'

Jennifer glanced at her watch. It wasn't even eight yet—her sister never saw this part of the day unless she was at school.

'Are you feeling all right?' she teased her, replacing the water bottle with a mug and pouring herself a coffee.

She frowned. 'Yeah— why?'

'You *do* know it's still your beauty sleep time?'

'Ha-ha, very funny, sis. You going to carry on taking the Mickey or be kind and pour me one of those?'

Jennifer laughed and poured her sister a coffee. 'Well, it's not like it's a school day.' She leant back against the counter-top and considered her over the cup. 'What has you up so early?'

Her sister looked away swiftly, her attention fixed on the fridge as she took out the milk. 'Want some?'

She offered it to her without meeting her eye and Jennifer shook her head, dread creeping up her spine. 'Kate…answer me.'

'Look, don't get mad, okay?'

She frowned, the dread becoming a full-blown chill. 'Tell me.'

'Mum has been caught wandering recently,' she said, slopping some milk into her mug, her nonchalance clearly forced.

'Wandering?' A lump wedged in her throat and she forced it down. 'How long has this been happening?'

'A couple of weeks—it tends to happen early in the morning, and when I ask her where she's going she says she's going to the office, to help Dad.'

'Kate, why haven't you said anything?'

'Because you have a lot going on and we've been managing okay.' Her sister slotted the milk back into the fridge and took up her mug, mimicking Jennifer's stance against the worktop.

'*We?*'

'Me and Mum's support workers.'

'But what about your studies? You have university coming up next year.'

'That's not a problem.' Kate gave an easy shrug. 'I'm going to study from home.'

Jennifer almost dropped her coffee. 'You're *what*?'

'Chill out, Jen. I can do what I want.'

'You *can't* want to study from home! Your grades are exceptional—you're Oxbridge material. You…you should be going off, living the student dream, studying hard, playing harder…' Her desperation to have her sister see sense had her words tripping over one another. 'You should be doing what *I* did.'

'It was different for you. *Mum* was different.' Her sister looked away, her determination giving way to sadness. 'I can't leave her now—who will look after her?'

Jennifer had known this day would come and she should have pre-empted Kate's decision, stopped her from making it in the first place. Time had crept up on her. Her sister was suddenly all grown up.

'It's not your responsibility,' she assured her. 'I will get more help in.'

'You know it's not that simple. Each new face only

unsettles Mum further, and it's good for her to have family around.'

There was no other family save her and her sister. There was no one else…

'Then I will be here more often.'

Kate looked to her in disbelief. 'How?'

'I should never have left you as much as I have.'

Guilt was her new default position, it seemed—if it wasn't Tony, it was her own family she was neglecting.

'I'm sorry—it wasn't fair. You've had to sacrifice your childhood to care for Mum while I've swanned off to London and lived out my dream.'

'Shut it!' snapped Kate, her coffee hitting the side and sloshing over the rim, her index finger wagging. 'Don't you *ever* apologise to me. You've done *everything* for us. If not for your career we would have nothing now. We wouldn't be able to stay in the house that Mum knows and loves. I wouldn't have university to look forward to, a car on the drive—a licence, even. Christ, you even pay the food bill.'

'I get all that, love, but seriously—if you don't go away to university I'll never forgive myself.'

'And I'll never forgive myself if you sacrifice your career for *me*.'

'I'm not talking about sacrificing my career.'

And she wasn't. Now that Marcus was on board anything was possible. It not only felt feasible from a business perspective for her to leave London more often, it also felt like a sound personal decision too. More space between them, more frequently. Then maybe her body would cease its crazy hedonistic craving for him and she could rein her heart back in.

Kate didn't look convinced. 'How would you make it work?'

'I have a new business partner now.'

Her sister's eyes narrowed on her. 'That wasn't expected, was it?'

'Hardly.'

'How come you didn't mention it last night?'

'It's complicated.'

'Complicated?' Kate nodded with interest. 'What's his name?'

'Who says it's a he?'

'Your secrecy, the way your voice has gone all funny and the way you've gone bright red… Need I go on?'

Damn it. 'Am I that obvious?'

''Fraid so,' she said, her eyes dancing. 'So come on—spill.'

'His name's Marcus.'

'Ooh, *Marcus*—nice name.'

She shot her sister a look and Kate immediately straightened, her fingers moving to her pursed lips and making a zip-like motion.

Jennifer rolled her eyes and continued. 'He already heads up several successful ventures, so I have complete faith that he will keep things ticking over if I were to split my time fifty-fifty between here and London. More if need—'

Her sister gave a dramatic yawn. '*Dull, dull, dull!* I meant, what's *he* like? There must be *something* about him if he's managed to get my unflappable sister's knickers in a twist.'

'He isn't doing anything with my knickers.' Her cheeks flushed over the outright lie and at her desire to have him play with them a hundred times over. 'And you're missing the point. Having Marcus means I can be at home more without jeopardising work.'

'But won't that mean time away from your hunky partner?'

'I didn't say he was hunky.'

'You didn't have to.'

'If you think teasing me about my new business partner is going to take the focus off you, missy, you're very much mistaken. University—you're going.'

Kate floundered before her.

'Look, you have to make your choices now, and you need to get it right. And, since I'm paying, I get a parental vote.' Her sister bristled a little at the last, but she continued. 'Besides, you won't leave for another year or so—plenty of time for me to take care of things operationally.'

Perhaps even move up north for good...

With a sigh, Kate picked up a cloth from the side and started to wipe up the coffee she had spilled.

Jennifer sipped her drink and said nothing, hoping the next words out of her sister's mouth would be the right ones.

'I'm not saying it's a definite yes,' she said eventually, 'but I'll think about it.'

Jennifer smiled. 'You'd better make it a definite yes, or I'm taking back that Mini Cooper you love so much.'

Kate visibly recoiled. 'You wouldn't?'

Her smile became a grin. She was happy to rib her sister a little. 'Wouldn't I...?'

'Just you try.' Kate waved the dirty cloth in the air

and stepped towards her. 'You want some coffee to mix in with that sweat, sis?'

Kate lunged for her and she squealed, making a break for it and doing her utmost not to spill her coffee in the process. 'Put that rag anywhere near me and the Cooper goes today.'

'Yeah, yeah—whatever you say.'

'I mean it.'

'Whatever,' her sister said, flouncing off to the sink and leaving Jennifer to head for her shower unscathed, her plan to put some much-needed distance between her and Marcus occupying her mind.

The question was, would he agree to it?

And would it be enough?

It turned out that the longest week had nothing on the weekend. Two days without her and Marcus had the oddest feeling of what it was like to actually miss someone.

He owed her. He'd spent two days playing the perfect grandson, making up for lost time, being ribbed by his grandmother and led astray by his grandfather down at the local pub. It had felt good. *Really* good. And some strange cloud had lifted over his past.

Still, none of it truly explained why he was currently standing outside King's Cross Station waiting for her train to come in. Not when he should be sitting at his desk getting some much-needed work done.

When Anna had told him Jennifer's train had been delayed, that she'd been stuck stationary for over an hour and was going out of her mind, he'd offered to collect her out of the goodness of his heart.

Whatever.

Yes, there'd been an element of that, but the truth came down to a multitude of reasons—some he barely understood. He wanted to thank her, he wanted to see her—badly—and he wanted her answer. He craved that above all else.

He prayed he'd imagined the weird mood she'd left in, but when Anna had told him she didn't want to be collected it had stirred up his worry and made him all the more determined to go.

And he'd not come empty-handed. She'd grumbled to Anna about the coffee on board and he'd already learnt how much she liked her caffeine fix. Cue him, two coffees in hand, his eyes skimming the crowd for her unmistakable red mane in the flurry of people.

He spotted her as soon as she emerged, her hair once more pinned up, her face distracted as she towered above the majority of those around her. And then she spotted him, her eyes narrowing, her face becoming set.

Ah, hell, she looked pissed off.

She wove through the masses towards him, her beige trench coat tied snugly to her waist, her jaw-dropping walk unhindered by the trolley suitcase she towed or the hefty handbag hooked over her shoulder.

'I told Anna to tell you not to come,' she said, as soon as she was within earshot.

He grinned. He couldn't help it. The fighter in her just got him every time. 'And *I* told Anna that it made sense for me to collect you—and you can't tell me you're not happy to see this.'

He held out the coffee and his keen eye detected

the minute semblance of a smile as she took it from him. 'On that you're right.'

She sounded weary, and now she was close he could see the shadows under her eyes, the stress lines he hadn't noticed before creasing her brow.

His grin became a frown. 'Are you okay?'

'I'm good,' she said, taking another sip. 'Or I will be when this caffeine takes effect.'

He didn't believe her. But standing outside a busy station trying to get to the bottom of it wasn't going to work.

'Here—let me take that.'

He moved to take her suitcase but she twisted to block him. 'I can manage just fine.'

'Ah, yes—sorry, I forgot.' He backed away, palms raised. 'Modern world and all that.'

She gave an unexpected laugh, the melodic sound warming him through—it felt good that he could still coax a laugh from her when she was clearly suffering in some way.

'Colin's not far away,' he said. 'Shall we go?'

'If you don't mind, I'd rather take a short walk first,' she said, her lids lowering as she faced the wind, one hand smoothing over her hair. 'After being stuck on that train I'd like to get some fresh air and stretch my legs.'

'Of course. We'll drop your bags with Colin on the way.'

'You don't need to come wi—'

He silenced her with a look. 'I could do with a walk too.'

'Fair enough,' she said, and her resigned expression worried him all the more.

'He's just over here.'

He looked away and started moving, trying to ignore the anxiety creeping its way in.

Colin straightened as they approached, a smile Marcus hadn't seen from him before breaking across his face.

'Good to see you, Miss Hayes, shall I take that?'

He reached out and she gave him a warm smile, passing him her bag. 'Thank you.'

'We're just going to take a walk,' Marcus said as Colin placed her bag in the boot. 'If you park up locally I'll call when we're done.'

'Very well, sir.'

He turned to offer her his arm, just as he'd done that first night, but her eyes darted away. It was a damn stupid move, really—they weren't on a date… they weren't even together. He morphed it into a gesture for her to precede him, and together they wove through the pedestrians, neither saying anything for a while.

'It's actually good that you've come,' she said eventually, giving him a sidelong glance.

'You've changed your tune,' he remarked, pulling his gaze up.

'It means we can discuss your proposition.'

It wasn't what he'd expected, but it worked for him. 'Sounds good to me.'

'Don't get too excited,' she said. 'It's a no.'

'A no?' He nodded thoughtfully, doing his best not to acknowledge the weird sensation pulling at his gut. 'Might I ask why?'

She looked at him, for longer this time, and then

she was off once more, picking up her pace. 'It's not easy to explain.'

'Okay,' he said, walking after her. 'Can you at least try?'

Again her eyes flicked back to his, but this time he could see wariness—fear, even—and she made no effort to elaborate.

'I'm going to get a complex if you keep this up.'

'*You* with a complex?' She rolled her eyes at him but her humour didn't reach her voice. 'If you say so.'

'Okay, it's true that I know from the way you climax when you're with me that it's not because you hate the sex.'

She let go of a breath, her eyes flickering, that knowing hint of colour hitting her cheeks. He'd done it on purpose—throwing her back into another time, another place.

'No, it's not that.'

Her husky intonation rippled through to his groin.

'Then you really *are* confusing me, because all I'm asking for is more of the same.'

She nodded. 'You're honest—I'll say that.'

'That's something you can always be certain of. Now, if you'll only do the same and put me out of my misery...'

'I don't have time for this between us.'

'What—sex? We've made a fair amount of time for it to date. Granted, not enough, but we can work on that.'

'No, not for sex.'

'Then I'm officially lost.'

She halted to look at him properly now, an unidentifiable emotion flaring in her eyes. 'It's everything else,' she said. 'We're meant to be *business* partners, doing what's best for the *business*. Not ourselves. But you dominate my every thought, whether we're together or not, and I can't give work the best of me when I'm so wrapped up in you. I can't sit in a business meeting, my entire focus on the job, when you are sitting right there with me, tempting my brain away.'

'Hey, it's been the same for me,' he said. 'It's precisely what I was saying in the car. Denying this between us only makes us distracted. I see us humouring this attraction as a way of keeping a lid on it, getting our heads back in the game...'

She studied him, and the pulse working in her throat, her clenched hold around her cup spoke volumes. 'This isn't some game.'

'Okay, sorry—I don't mean it flippantly,' he backpedalled. 'I just mean that it'll help us to concentrate, to focus again.'

'And then what?'

'What do you mean?'

'When you've had your fill? What happens then?'

He shrugged, confusion reigning. 'We'll deal with that when we get to it.'

She shook her head at him, a strange smile quirking her lips. 'If only life was as simple as you make it out to be.'

'It *can* be that simple.'

'Not for me,' she said, pressing on once more without giving him a backward glance. 'It's too risky— *you're* too risky—and I have enough to worry about with my sister leaving for university soon and my mother's health declining.'

'I'm sorry to hear that.'

She ignored the way his concern warmed her, the way it urged her to look at him. She knew it would break her resolve and she spun on her heel, eyes averted. 'Look, let's get back to the office—we've lost enough of the day as it is.'

'But we haven't finished our talk.'

'Yes, we have,' she said, starting to retrace their steps without waiting for him. 'I don't have time for a relationship.'

He fell into step beside her. 'And I'm not asking for a relationship.'

'No, sorry—I forgot.' She shot him a look. 'You're just asking for some *mutual fun*.'

The way she said it messed with his head, and something inside him turned desperate. *Was she looking for more? Was that where he'd gone wrong?*

But what did it matter if she was? It sure as hell wasn't what *he* wanted, was it?

She was still charging ahead, and the sudden need to have her undivided attention had him tossing his coffee into a nearby bin and cutting off her stride. He pulled her into a deserted side-street and spun her to face him.

'Tell me this isn't fun for you,' he said. 'Tell me you don't *want* me and I'll drop this.'

'Marcus.' The way she said it—breathless, almost fearful—made his body ache.

She looked up at him, her green eyes wide, and he stepped forward, forcing her back.

'Tell me this isn't explosive.'

She shook her head, pressing her free hand feebly against him. *'Marcus.'*

'Tell me it doesn't make your heart beat uncontrollably, your blood ring in your ears and your sanity leave you.'

He continued walking her backwards as he raised his hand to cup her chin. 'Tell me it doesn't take it all away—the stress, the pain, the worry.'

He could feel her wavering, feel her trembling beneath his touch. 'Please let me be your escape.'

It was what *he* wanted—so much it scared him—and he dropped his head, pulling at her lower lip with his teeth, taking it back to the sexual, back to the comfortable.

'Let me drive you wild…let me make you wet.'

She gasped, her back hitting the shielded recess of a fire escape. 'Marcus, we're *outside*. There are *people*.'

'No one can see us here,' he whispered against her parted lips, getting off on knowing the busy bustle of the street was within earshot and feeling her imminent surrender. 'And I can't wait any longer. I need to know—are you wet for me?'

She shook her head, clamping her eyes shut.

'Liar.'

'Please,' she whispered, her eyes lifting to his, and he paused.

She wanted him—he could see it burning in her gaze, in the hand that grasped his chest, pulling him closer. *Damn it, she probably didn't even know she was doing it.*

'Tell me, you don't want me right now and I will stop.'

His cock pressed painfully against his fly, against

her, but he *would* back away—it would kill him, but he'd do it.

'I... I—'

She broke off, shaking her head as though she couldn't believe her own mind, her tongue brushing nervously across her lower lip. 'I can't.'

'Can't?' he pressed, hope surging.

'I want you.'

It was hushed, it was uncertain, but it was there. A groan ripped through his restraint, and his lips crushed hers with every possessive ounce of his being.

Coffee and lip gloss invaded his tastebuds, its effect like a drug. Her mouth relented to the force of his, her blissful whimper singing through him as heat coursed through his blood.

He heard the sound of her cup hitting the ground, felt heat against his leg as the liquid seeped into his trousers but he didn't care.

'Marcus...' she moaned, raking a hand through his hair as her other hand clawed at him through his jacket.

'This kind of fun is worth fighting for,' he rasped.

Their mouths collided, their kiss spiralling out of control, their tongues exploring one another with invasive delight; twisting, probing, desperate for more. His cock was practically bursting on that alone, and then she buried her head in his neck.

'I'm losing it.'

'Not yet, you're not.'

His hands dropped to her waist and he yanked the tie of her trench coat undone. He reached for her thighs, coaxing her skirt up, desperate to seek her out.

He slipped a hand between her legs, felt the wet fabric of her knickers greeting him. '*Fuck*, Jennifer.'

She clung to his shoulders, her body arching to grant him access, and he slid inside. She was so warm, so inviting, and he buried his fingers in her, pulling back to slide them over her clit. She bucked against him, her teeth biting into his skin as she suppressed a cry, their public location clearly not lost on her.

He circled over her, gently at first, loving the way she undulated against his touch, and then faster, harder, in time with her breathing. Her tension mounted—he could feel it in every rigid line of her body as he pressed against her. And as she rocked against him forcefully, her climax claiming her, he covered her mouth with his own, drowning out her cry, swallowing it as her entire body shattered against him.

It was swift, it was brief, it was soul-crushing. And the shift in the atmosphere from mind-obliterating lust to heavy regret was sudden and disorientating.

Quietly she buried her head in his shoulder, normalising her breathing, and he extracted his hand, careful not to leave a trace on the fabric of her suit.

He planted his hands either side of her as she straightened, her eyes downcast, her fingers trembling as she smoothed her clothing back into place and re-tied her coat.

He wanted to say something—anything. He just didn't know what.

'We shouldn't have done that,' she said quietly.

Her words from the car played back to him. 'Not this again.'

She sent him a look and his frustration died, guilt

crushing him. 'I'm sorry. I just needed you to remember what it's like—what it could still be like.'

She held his eyes, her expression one of such misery it pulled him apart. 'Please, Marcus, if you care for me in any way, promise me this will stop.'

He took hold of her upper arms, his thumbs stroking her coat, his caress aimed to soothe and reassure. 'I'm not asking for a relationship.'

'Don't you *get* it?' she blurted, her eyes glistening. 'I can't keep having sex with you without *wanting* one.'

The tightness twisted him up inside. *She wants more.*

'I can see you understand,' she said, her eyes skimming his face, turning hard. 'So promise me?'

He released her, raking an unsteady hand through his hair as he struggled to take it in.

'Promise?' she pressed.

'Okay, okay—I promise.' He was barely aware of the words coming out of his mouth, so lost was he in her revelation.

'Good.'

She stepped out of his hold, and through the haze he could see her composure falling into place.

'I think some space will do us good,' she said, looking over to where the alley met the main street. 'With Mum's health on the decline, I'm going to be needed at home more.'

He frowned at her. 'In Yorkshire?'

'Yes.' She nodded calmly, without looking back. 'I need to take the pressure off my sister and make sure she gets her education.'

Slowly he nodded, but the twisted feeling in his

gut was getting worse. He'd called it fun, just sex, so why did her refusal disturb him so much? Was it because she wanted more? Or because she was intending to be away more?

Christ, he had no clue.

'How often do you need to go back?' he asked tonelessly.

'I don't know.'

She shrugged, and her poise was starting to grate against the loss of his own.

'Fifty-fifty split, I think.'

He nodded, the impact of her words sinking in. 'Of course you must go if they need you.'

He suddenly felt like an utter shit. Here he was, pursuing her, when she clearly had bigger things to worry about.

He should be grateful he was avoiding that future complication too.

So why did it feel as if his worst nightmare was coming true?

He thrust a shaky hand through his hair. The rollercoaster inside his head was scaring him.

'Let's go.' He forced himself to move forward, to head for the high street, and she stepped into line beside him. 'We can discuss a strategy to make the split work on the return journey.'

'Thank you.'

He sent her a sidelong glance, looking for the emotion he'd witnessed not five minutes before. But there was nothing.

He had to admire her for that.

And it was time he did the same. He'd do what he should've done ages ago and sort out a date elsewhere, hope the distraction would help him live up to his promise and leave her the hell alone.

It was time to stop behaving like a love-sick puppy.

Love?

Where the fuck had that *come from?*

CHAPTER FOURTEEN

A FULL TWO weeks had passed since the alley incident—since Marcus had promised he would leave her alone, and she'd confessed her desire for more and scared him off entirely.

And the greater the distance he put between them, the greater was her need to have him back, to accept what little he was able to give—because the current situation was unbearable.

The change in him drove her crazy. He communicated via email, even when a simple conversation would have been quicker and easier. When she forced him to talk he rarely looked her way. In the few meetings they attended together his attention was on everyone else.

It wasn't that he was rude. Not at all. He was businesslike, platonic—everything she'd asked for.

And she hated it.

Then there was her goal to split her time fifty-fifty. It was feasible, but her worry over letting go had had her upping her efforts to the point of exhaustion, convinced that putting in the extra time would ensure her handle on the company didn't slip. Not for anything. Or anyone.

As for her feelings—they would go with time. They had to.

Planting her elbows on the desk, she massaged her temples and pushed through the mind fog, the emotional turmoil. She had work to get done. It was long past home-time and she was poring over financial projections that she should have finished reviewing hours ago. She squinted at the figures. The computer screen and her desk lamp offered the only light since the main office was dark and deserted.

Half an hour later she was reviewing her feedback when her office was lit up, by light leaking in from the main office outside.

Heart in her mouth, she glanced up.

Who'd be here at this hour?

Marcus.

Her pulse took charge and did its thing, and her body tripped out at the mere sight of him. As much as she tried to force it down, it just kept on coming. The feeling of being ignored for the best part of a fortnight only served to intensify it all.

Would he ignore her now, when he realised that she was still here? That she was the only one here?

To her surprise, he didn't head to his office—he strode straight for hers.

Definitely not ignoring her, then...

Slowly she got to her feet, readying herself for his proximity, searching for what to say and the numerous reasons he might be here.

She walked to her door, reaching it at the same time as he did.

His eyes raked over her, something close to anger sparking in their depths. *What was wrong now?*

Cautious, she swung it open. 'Hey.'

'Hey, yourself,' he said, his mouth returning to form a grim line.

'What are you doing here?'

'I was about to ask you the same thing.'

She brushed her hand over her hair. 'I've yet to leave.'

'Yeah, I got that much.' He looked to the empty office and then to her desk, covered in various papers and several coffee cups. 'You know, it's not good to work this late.'

'What can I say? I'm a workaholic.'

'Tell me something I don't know.' He sounded beat, and his eyes returned to her with a frown. 'It's been every night for the last two weeks, though. It's not sustainable.'

'I have things to get done.'

'Those *"things"* can wait until tomorrow.'

'Not these.'

'*Christ*, Jennifer.' He thrust his hand through his hair. 'What is this about? You can't always work like this.'

He was concerned for her wellbeing. It was obvious now. And it warmed her through, its effect as powerful as the desire she so missed. She liked it that he cared, regardless of whether it was wise or not.

She gave a small smile. 'I'm more used to it than you know.'

'But you've done your father proud already. You don't need to keep on pushing—'

'This is not about my father,' she interjected without thinking. A strange softening sensation curled its way in—he'd listened to her, really *listened*.

'Then what is it?'

He leant against the doorframe, his frown deepening, his presence dominating her vision and the scent of freshly applied aftershave filling the air. Suddenly she felt inadequate. Her hair was falling out of its bun, and her dress was crumpled from her sitting down for the best part of a day. God knew what she smelt like. And now he was asking why she was like this. *Why?*

She bit into her bottom lip. *Because of you!* she wanted to scream. *Because you can't offer me more.*

'Tell me,' he said, pushing off the doorframe and closing the gap between them. 'I'm worried it's because you think you're somehow giving up by leaving—'

'I'm *not* leaving,' she cut in. 'I'll be just as present from my desk up north.'

'Okay.' His eyes widened, his palms raised outwards. 'I meant splitting your time between Yorkshire and here.'

She crossed her arms around her middle, not liking the unease creeping in. 'It's doable.'

'I agree—it is.' He nodded. 'But I worry you're having trouble believing it.'

'I believe it just fine,' she said, shaking her head and feeling her hair falling across her face. She saw him move to touch it and backed away.

'Sorry.' He bowed his head, raising his hand to rub at the bridge of his nose instead, his stress permeating the air.

Should she say something? Anything? Like, It's okay?

But it wasn't.

He took a long, drawn-out breath, lowering his hand as he lifted his gaze to her. 'Then is it me?'

She froze, her cheeks chilling, his accurate conclusion startling her. 'I've always worked hard.'

'I know.' His eyes pierced her, their depths earnest, deep with concern. 'But I feel like this is different, like I'm somehow to blame.'

'Marcus, don't flatter yourself,' she blustered, raising her chin. 'I'm working because I want to.'

He looked as if he would argue further, and she spoke over him.

'And the sooner you leave, the sooner I can finish and get off home.'

'Have you at least eaten?'

She blushed. She knew she didn't look after herself, and him pointing out the obvious made her feel doubly foolish. 'I'll get something shortly. What about you? You look like you're off out.'

His eyes wavered. 'I'm meeting up with an old friend.'

'Old friend' sounded like code for old flame.

She itched to ask, and hated herself for it, turning away instead. 'Well, don't let me keep you.'

He reached out for her arm, the warmth of his fingers permeating the thin fabric of her dress and she caught her breath, her eyes flicking questioningly to his.

'Promise me, you'll leave soon.'

She'd had the ridiculous notion he was going to pull her into him, kiss her, anything but his concerned plea. Disappointment clogged up her throat, clipping at her words, 'I'll leave when I'm ready.'

She pulled away and headed to the desk. The lack

of movement behind her telling of his hesitation and she lifted a document, any document, throwing her focus into it.

'Fair enough,' he said eventually, his voice disturbingly raw. 'I guess I'll see you in the morning.'

'Uh-huh,' she murmured, her eyes fixed on the page of swimming grey, her ears attuned to his every sound.

She listened to him walk away, not daring to turn, not wanting to watch him go, scared that the tears she didn't want to shed would start to fall.

What the hell was he doing?

Opposite him, his ex Zara was discussing food with the waiter, her pregnancy making her extra-cautious with her choices, and he was using the time to berate his idiotic move.

He should never have gone into the office—never asked that Colin drive by the building on the way to the restaurant. He just hadn't been able to leave well alone.

And yet he'd done everything she'd asked of him, fought every urge to see her to ensure he stood by his promise. His conscience should be clear. Even if it hurt…even if it felt wrong.

But tonight he'd had the urge to check that she'd gone home. She was losing weight, the worry lines and dark shadows on her face ever-present, and it was pulling him apart inside. When he'd seen her light on he'd been determined to get her to leave.

Only the main office had been deserted, just the two of them in the entire space, and his restraint had hung dangerously in the balance. And instead of doing

what he'd intended he'd annoyed the hell out of her.
Idiot.

'Sir, what can I get you?'

The waiter looked at him and he stared unsee-
ingly at the menu, ordering his usual dish and passing
the menu back. The idea of eating when Jennifer so
clearly wouldn't plagued him. He should send Colin
with something. At least then he would know she'd
eaten.

Zara smiled at him, her cheeks glowing. Pregnancy
clearly suited her. 'So, to what do I owe this unexpected pleasure?'

Hell, he didn't know. He could hardly say he'd
needed to get out but he didn't do lads' drinks and
he couldn't do dates. Not any more.

'I had some time on my hands.'

She laughed, her blonde hair bobbing, blue eyes
twinkling. 'You with time on your hands? Impossible.'

He smiled. She was right there.

'You look well.'

'Is that you changing the subject?'

'Maybe.'

Her smile grew, one hand dropping to stroke over
her bump. 'I am well,' she said. 'I never thought I was
the maternal type. It's funny what love can do to you.'

Love. There was that word again.

'I'm glad. You were always too good for me.'

Her eyes narrowed. 'I don't think that was ever
the case.'

'No?'

He didn't believe her—not in the slightest. But he
wasn't the same man he'd been then. He could feel it.
His concern for Jennifer told him as much.

Bloody Jennifer—she needed to eat.
'Hold that thought.'
He took up his mobile and issued Colin with a text.

Check she's still at work. If she is, take her food. She won't say no to you.

She'd kill him. But he didn't care.

He placed his mobile back down and looked at Zara with fresh eyes. She was beautiful, she was clever, and they'd got along well. So how come she'd never got under his skin in the same way?

'Why didn't we work out?'

Her eyes widened, and he couldn't blame her. He'd never indulged in the personal—not when it came to conversation—not until Jennifer.

'What? You mean besides the fact you always told me you didn't want anything serious?'

'Besides that.'

She took a sip of water, her eyes assessing him. 'You want the truth?'

He nodded. 'The whole ugly lot.'

'I never felt like you were fully *with* me,' she said softly, her gaze reminiscent. 'Your mind was always on the next big project, your next acquisition, your next whatever. You couldn't live in the moment and I couldn't compete with it.'

He let her words sink in, comparing them to how he felt when he was with Jennifer, how he wanted to draw out each and every moment, how she filled his mind whether he was with her or not…

'It's far easier to cope with you being distracted when we're just friends.'

His phone buzzed with a reply from Colin. He was on it.

'Take now, for example.' She gestured to his phone. 'Another big project, by any chance?'

He met her eyes, the answer sticking in his throat, and her brow furrowed with his hesitation. 'It's not, is it?'

He shook his head.

'Well, I'll be…' she said, a grin breaking across her face with dawning realisation. 'Someone's managed to crack the great Marcus Wright.'

Crack?

It wasn't a bad way to put it. He certainly felt as if someone had ripped him apart and put him back together all wrong. 'It seems that way.'

'Now, *this* I have to hear.' Zara settled back into her seat, making herself nice and comfortable.

'Why do I get the feeling you're going to take some weird twisted delight in this?'

'Not at all, Marcus,' she said softly. 'It's high time you realised everyone deserves a piece of happiness—including you.'

As the outer office lit up again Jennifer's heart leapt. When she saw Colin striding towards her, takeaway bag in hand, her tummy did a weird dance of disappointment and pleasure.

Marcus had sent her food. He cared enough to make sure she ate.

She beckoned Colin in and he opened the door.

'From Mr Wright,' he said, walking in and depositing the bag on the desk before her.

'You shouldn't have gone to so much trouble,'

she said, but she opened the bag with glee, glancing inside. The smell of Chinese food wafted up to her and her tummy rumbled in excited protest. 'It smells lovely.'

'There's a mixture—hopefully something you like.' He shifted awkwardly on his feet. 'I would have asked you first, but...'

'But you knew I'd refuse?'

'Something like that.'

She gave him a reassuring smile. 'Well, it's just what I need. Thank you.'

She expected him to turn and leave but he still stood there, doing that weird uncomfortable dance. 'Is there something else?'

'Aye, I'm to wait and give you a chance to eat,' he said, moving to clasp his hands in front of him as he stilled. 'Then I'm to take you home.'

She coloured. *Really? A bloody chaperone?*

But there was no use arguing. Not with Colin, at any rate.

And, hell, the truth was Marcus was right. She did need to eat, and she did need to go home.

It would just be easier to accept if she knew her unoccupied mind wouldn't be filled with *him*.

It was late when he bade Zara goodnight. The evening had been good for him. In a way it had been good for her too. It had been like some weird closure for her to see him so wrapped up in someone.

And he truly was wrapped up—in deep, over his head. Whatever way he looked at it he was falling for her. *Hell, he already had.*

But what did he do with that? It was one thing to

realise he was capable of love, to accept it was too late to shield himself. It was another to know what to do with it.

Right from the outset he'd never stood a chance. The moment she'd come into his life his world had changed. And so had he. She'd opened his eyes to how his life could be if he let go of his past.

But he was still scared. Scared of what would happen if he let those feelings take hold, risked it all to tell her and ask her to take a chance on him.

The question plagued him. *What if he lost her?*

The very idea winded him. Yes, he'd parked his past, but it had still moulded him, left ingrained in him the life lesson of love ripped away.

How did he unlearn that?

CHAPTER FIFTEEN

NO, NO, NO, NO, NO!

Jennifer stared at her mobile news feed, her coffee and toast forgotten, her freshly showered hair dripping over the reports she'd brought home after her impromptu Chinese takeaway the previous night. She ignored them now, the news taking all her attention.

Despite their best efforts, their US competitor had beaten them to their product launch.

Marcus was going to be pissed off. Hell, she *was pissed off. Had she made the right call? Fuck, would he blame her?*

Leaving her breakfast untouched, she raced upstairs, pulled on a pair of trousers and a polo neck, plaited her hair and applied some gloss to her lips.

That would have to do.

Grabbing her mobile, she hit the stairs and issued a hurried text to Marcus.

Work emergency. Need to talk asap.

It was six a.m. *He had to be up, right?*

If he didn't reply by the time she got to the office

then she'd ring him until he did. The situation was still salvageable. She knew it. She just needed him to know it too.

When she arrived the foyer was deserted, save for the security guard. She greeted him and took the lift to her floor. She knew someone was in because she'd seen the lights of the main office from outside.

It had to be him. Who else would be in at this time?

The usual rush had her pulse skipping and she breathed through it.

It wouldn't always be this hard—it couldn't be…

Exiting the lift, she looked towards his office. The lights were on behind his blinds.

Definitely him, then.

Her tummy somersaulted and she ignored it, shrugging off her coat and heading straight to her office. She dumped her belongings and immediately left for his.

The noise of him moving around reached her. Her tummy was taking on the feats of an Olympic gymnast but she fought it.

She rapped on his door and, swinging it open, strode straight in. 'Marc—'

The remainder of his name died on a gasp and her legs halted mid-stride, an instant fire making further somersaults in her stomach impossible. He was standing in the open doorway to his bathroom, his virtually naked rear glistening with an indecent strip of towel slung low about his waist…

He started to turn towards her and she twirled on her heel, cheeks burning. '*So* sorry.'

'Hey, easy,' he said, his husky intonation teasing

every rigid stretch of her body. 'I think you've seen enough of me before not to get bashful all of a sudden.'

'Sorry, I should've knocked properly—should've waited. I shouldn't… I just didn't expect… Well, I didn't think you'd be so…*naked*,' she babbled, standing at the doorway to his office, needing to move through it yet finding herself rooted.

'I wasn't expecting anyone to be in yet.'

She bit into her bottom lip. She could hear him moving behind her, and the urge to look was driving her crazy. *Just one glance…*

'Granted, having seen the news this morning, I should've expected you to be.'

'Uh-huh.' It was all that could come out, and was high-pitched as it was. She should leave him to get dressed. Their conversation could wait that long, at least. She moved away from the door. 'I'll just—'

'Did you see what the press are saying about it?' He talked over her, and his tone and topic drew her in.

'Not yet.'

'Take a look at this.'

Her eyes wavered between the doorway and him, without truly focusing on either. She needed to get past this. *She* was the one who had said no more sex, but, Christ, she'd hardly expected to find him half naked…*again*.

Forcing herself, she turned and headed to where he was bent over his desk, one hand hovering over his trackpad, one finger pointing at the screen.

She fixed her gaze on where his finger rested, doing her damnedest to ignore the steamy male scent and the inviting warmth radiating off him.

She planted her hands on the cold glass desktop and read. And then she read some more. But the words weren't going in. She couldn't set her focus, her head going dizzy with his appeal.

He straightened on a sigh, and she caught sight of his chest flexing as he did so, which sent desire climbing up her throat.

He was less than an arm's reach away. *Why couldn't she just give in?*

And then came the painful retort *He can't love you back*—and she almost choked with it.

Love? Was that where she was at?

'What do you think?' he asked.

'Think…?' *Get with it, Jennifer.*

She swallowed and he coughed. She glanced at him and caught a brief sweep of his tensed muscles, his heated gaze, and knew he wanted her.

But he doesn't want more.

It served to up her resolve. 'I have some ideas.'

'Ideas?'

'Yes.' Pulling her plait over her shoulder, she righted herself and turned to face him fully. 'Why don't you get dressed and join me in my office?'

He brushed a hand over his hair, sweeping the damp curls away from his face and she almost snapped, almost reached up to repeat his exact move.

She fisted her hands at her sides. 'Unless you want to do this half-naked?'

He gave her a lop-sided grin. 'I will if you will!'

'Marcus.' She whirled away and threw her hands in the air, her sexual frustration and teetering resolve sending her storming for the door. 'My office—when you've bothered to put some clothes on.'

* * *

He would have laughed if he hadn't been working so damn hard to appear normal.

Seeing her, knowing now how he felt, had intensified every sensation. When he'd heard her say his name his heart had ballooned, cutting off his ability to breathe. And then he'd seen her, his eyes devouring every last inch of her, and his towel had been lucky to stay steady.

It was fortunate that he hadn't just kissed the look of shock right off her face. The hint of lip gloss glistening on her otherwise innocently bare features had pleaded with him to do as much. Her woven hair, still wet, told of a recent shower, and the thought of her in it, naked and slick, had teased him senseless.

And if someone had told him he'd find a polo neck and trousers sexy he would've laughed them out of the room.

In the bathroom he hit the cold tap, turning it on full, and doused his face, trying to send a message to the searing burn making camp in his gut.

The thing was, if it was *just* that—desire—then he would be able to cope. He knew he would. It was the fact it was so much more than desire now. Seeing her and knowing that left him all kinds of vulnerable, and it was chewing him up inside.

He'd barely slept the night before, battling with it all, the risk weighing heavy on him. But he couldn't carry on like this. He knew that now. He just had to work out how to broach the subject and not send her running for the hills with his turnaround.

He raked the towel over himself and got dressed, prepping his mind for the topic at hand—the competitor's product launch. They would deal with that and then he would make sense of the rest.

He found her at her desk, scribbling furiously on her notepad. The professional Jennifer he had come to know so well was in full swing. She was every bit the businesswoman he had come to respect above all others, her brain working like no one else's he knew, piecing things together even quicker than him—and that, frankly, was saying something.

'I see you really *do* have some ideas.'

She glanced up, her eyes bright with excitement.

'I do—check this out.'

She beckoned him over, moving so she could stand directly behind her and could read what she was working on.

'I think our product is better,' she said. 'I've taken a look at what they're offering and ours outstrips it by far.'

'Okay…' he said, his hands sinking forcibly into his pockets.

'I told you it was a good idea to merge product specifications!'

She was ribbing him, but all he felt was pride blooming. He had the crazy urge to pull her into his arms and tell her as much.

'So, I reckon the best solution,' she continued, 'is to have a red carpet affair for our launch and do it now.'

'Now?'

'Well, not literally—but certainly within the next week or two, hot on the back of this. I think I can pull a few strings, get some big names in the business to attend, bring in the press, and it'll bury this morning's news.'

He chuckled. 'Remind me never to get on your bad side.'

She smiled up at him, her expression unreadable. 'Our product *is* better,' she stressed. 'It deserves to be treated as such.'

'No arguments here.'

Her eyes went back to the page and she traced her index finger down the list she'd created. 'These are my first thoughts on guests, location, theme, catering and—'

The trill of his phone interrupted, but it was a while before he even registered it because he was so lost in her and what she was saying.

'Do you want to get that?'

Her question brought with it his senses. Of course he should get it. Someone ringing at this hour had to be important. He slid his phone out of his pocket and checked the ID. *Gran.*

He stared at it, a thread of unease coiling steadily up his spine.

'Who is it?'

He could hear the concern in her voice. *She was so astute.*

'It's my grandmother.' *Or would it be Pops again?*

He knew he needed to answer but his fingers were frozen around the phone. If he didn't answer, whatever news was coming wouldn't be real...

Christ, don't be ridiculous!

Next to him, Jennifer stood and placed a hand on his arm. 'Would you like me to step out?'

The comfort of her touch radiated through the ice and his fingers came alive. 'No.'

She nodded and he answered the call, lifting the phone to his ear. 'Gran?'

'Marcus.'

'Pops?' It came out gruff, unrecognisable even to his own ears.

'She's been rushed in—'

His grandfather broke off and Marcus felt as if someone had a noose around his neck, was pulling it tight, his very life being squeezed out of him.

He needed to speak, but the words weren't coming. He shut his eyes, then opened them to seek out Jennifer, and she was there, her own eyes shining with an emotion that he knew mirrored his own.

He burned to reach for her but didn't dare. And then she was doing it—slipping her arms around him, tucking her head beneath his chin, and his breath was freed up, leaving him in a rush.

Thank you, he wanted to say. But his free arm closed around her instead, taking the strength she offered, the comfort, the love... *If only.*

His grandfather coughed. 'Sorry, son.'

'It's okay, Pops, tell me what's happened?'

He heard him take a shaky breath and then he was rambling—something about another stroke, her being in critical care, the doctor's current assessment...

It was all coming at him in a blur, but he knew he needed to get moving—he needed to be there *now.*

'Okay, Pops, listen.' The words came out controlled, and for that he was grateful. He wanted to reassure him, no matter what was going on inside himself. His grandfather needed his strength. 'I can be with you in a few hours. I'll check flights or I'll drive. Either way I'll be with you by lunchtime.'

His grandfather let go of another shaky breath, 'Thank you, son.'

'I'll see you soon.'

Marcus cut the call and sucked in some much-needed air, feeling Jennifer tighten her arms around him as he let it out.

'How bad is it?' she asked softly.

'She's in critical care,' he said, his skin prickling as his gut rolled. 'Another stroke.'

'I'm so sorry, Marcus.'

She lifted her head off his chest to look up at him, and there was so much compassion in her gaze that he could almost—*almost*—believe she loved him too. That there was already so much more between them.

He searched her face, wanting to ask, wanting to confess.

'Go now,' she said. 'I'll get the launch finalised, and if you can't make it, it doesn't matter.'

He nodded, knowing she spoke sense but feeling rooted to the spot, rooted to *her*.

'And if you can make it, all you need to do is turn up and do what you do best—schmooze.'

'Schmooze?' He gave her a wry smile. 'Is that all I'm good for?'

'Maybe…' she teased gently.

God, he wanted to keep hold of her, take her with him. The weirdest feeling took hold—that nothing could hurt too deeply if she was near.

'Go on, Marcus, be there for your family.' She stepped back and paused, her eyes flickering, and then she swept her arms around him once more, raising herself up to say against his ear, 'Know that I am here for you if you need me.'

She turned into him, her lips pressing softly into his cheek, and the world stopped, warmth flooding him as his love for her swelled.

And then she was gone, dropping back as a shutter fell over her expression, wrapping her arms around her middle. 'Let me know when you get there safely?'

'I will.'

He had to fight not to pull her back, to make her kiss much more than a peck, but the moment was so special, so right, he didn't want to break it.

Slipping his phone into his pocket, he headed for the door, pausing on the threshold to give her one last look. 'Thank you.'

And then he left, with the chill resurfacing, increasing with every step he took away from her.

Jennifer watched him go, her insides trembling as she fought the desire to follow.

He'd needed her—she'd seen it in him. She didn't know what it meant but it had called to her. It still did. It had been emotional rather than physical, and had he said *Come with me* she knew beyond a doubt that she would have gone.

But he hadn't, and she hadn't expected him to—not really. So she would help in the one way she knew how: she would keep on top of work and make sure he wasn't disturbed. She would field his calls, organise the best product launch he'd ever seen, and work every waking moment.

She knew she wasn't being entirely selfless, that it would help her too—because being awake and busy meant not thinking about the mess her heart had become. And, no matter what she'd seen in him today, it didn't negate what he had said to her previously.

She'd come so close to blurting *I love you*—had felt it on the tip of her tongue as she'd drowned in his agonised gaze. The only thing to stop it had been the memory of his obvious horror when she'd hinted at wanting more in the alley.

But for the briefest moment she'd believed he felt it too, that something had changed between them.

Was it too much to hope for?

The fear-filled flutter in her belly kick-started and she pushed her mind to work.

Concentrate on something you're good at—something you can control...something that doesn't ache as if it's never going to stop...

CHAPTER SIXTEEN

WHEN HE CLIMBED into bed that night, absolutely wiped out, he expected sleep to come quickly. He should've known better. As soon as his head hit the pillow his thoughts turned to Jennifer.

He smiled as he remembered his grandmother's face when he'd told her about Jennifer. His intention had been to distract her from the tubes and the machines beeping around them; what he'd got had been a lecture.

'Don't let this woman slip through your fingers,' she'd told him. 'If you don't try you'll wonder forever, and life's far too short for that.'

Having those words uttered in a hospital, in a building so full of loss, his own deep-rooted argument had collided with hers. Yes, you could have a long and happy life together, just as his grandparents had proved, or by some mean twist of fate it could be taken away from you far too early, like his parents.

But the idea of not trying for the former, of letting Jennifer go, was agony in itself.

He rolled over and picked up his mobile from the bedside table. Propping himself up on his elbow, he scanned his messages. He'd had several from her throughout the day. They'd all contained work updates, but he'd sensed her intention had really been to check on him. The fact that she cared was obvious and it gave him hope.

Another message came through.

How's your gran?

Doing well, all things considered.

Thank goodness. And you?

Missing you. He wanted to type it so badly, but not yet. It wasn't right.

I'm okay. You should get some sleep.

Yes, boss.

His smile grew.

Night.

Night. x

The 'x' heated him through, and without thinking he sent a simple 'x' back.

He stared at it, at the harmless letter glowing and pulsing at him from her message to him.

Hope swelled.

He stayed just over a week—until the day of the launch...until he was certain his grandmother was going to be okay.

He stopped by the hospital on his way home. The beeping machines were thankfully long gone, and his grandmother's new private room was cosy, with splashes of yellow, and the flowers he'd brought her lit up the window ledge.

'You're stubborn, my boy—remember that.' She positively beamed up at him. 'Don't you be taking no for an answer.'

He chuckled and bent to press a kiss to her brow. 'I'll try not to. But she can be rather stubborn too.'

'Good—I like a girl with a bit of backbone.'

'Oh, I have no doubt you'll like her.'

'Well, make sure you bring her home soon, so we can see for ourselves.' Sadness swept across her features. 'I often worried that you would never settle… that somehow your past had seen to that.'

'Hey, easy, Gran.' He placed a hand over hers. 'It just took me a while, that's all.'

She nodded, her eyes glittering with a smile, and his throat tightened.

'We understood why you didn't come home much. We knew how hard it was for you to keep coming back here.'

'Don't make excuses for me.' He squeezed her palm. 'I should've come back more. I was being selfish— foolish, even.'

'It's not foolish to want to avoid those memories.' She took a shaky breath. 'Nonetheless, the past is the past, darling. You can't change it, but you shouldn't let it taint your future either.'

'I know,' he said softly. 'I get that now.'

'Aren't you done lecturing the boy yet, Angie?'

His grandfather's booming Welsh lilt invaded the room as he joined them, a fresh bouquet in his arms.

'I don't *lecture*,' his grandmother bristled.

'Whatever you say, dear.' He smiled and bowed down to plant a kiss upon her forehead, adding with a wink, 'The important thing is, did it work?'

She returned his smile, happiness filling her cheeks with colour. 'How could you ever doubt me?'

His grandfather chuckled and looked to Marcus, his gaze warm and hopeful. 'You finally ready to stop running and start living?'

Marcus grinned, loving their interchange, and loving the whole promise life suddenly held. 'You'd better believe it, Pops.'

'Diolch i'r Arglwydd.'

His grandfather pounded him jovially on the back, back to his best now that Gran was on the mend.

'So what are you waiting for? Be off with you and bring us back a granddaughter-in-law.'

'I'll do my damnedest.'

'Language!' came his grandmother's warning.

He exchanged a look with his grandfather and they both erupted with laughter.

'He has you to thank for that, Angie.'

She gave an exaggerated huff. 'I have no idea what you're talking about.'

'Whatever, Gran,' he teased. 'I'll see you both soon—*very soon*.'

And he would. He could say it and mean it now.

Over a week had gone by in a crazy, manic blur. During the week Jennifer had thrown herself into work, and at the weekend she'd thrown herself into her family. But in between she'd thought of *him*.

They'd exchanged messages regarding work and she'd asked after his grandmother. And as time had gone on she'd started to doubt what she thought she'd seen in his face, what she thought she'd felt change between them, and her hope had slowly died. Even the 'x' had become a distant memory.

It was now launch night and here she was, supposed to be getting ready, but her tummy was in knots. She knew that he would be here soon, that she would see him again, but she didn't know how to react, how to feel.

She frowned into her bathroom mirror, her unmade-up face staring back at her. She was going to have to do something. The shadows beneath her eyes spoke of sleep deprivation, and her pale and hollow cheeks were the result of her non-existent appetite.

'It's not going to make itself look good, you know,' came Anna's softly spoken remark through the open doorway, and her smile was one of concern. 'You want me to help?'

Jennifer ignored her question and tightened the belt on her dressing gown. 'How long do we have?'

Anna glanced at the mobile in her hand. 'Taxi's due in an hour.'

'Have you heard from Marcus?'

'Not recently, but he—' She broke off as her mobile started to ring. 'Ah—one sec… Hello?' she said wandering off, phone to her ear.

Jennifer looked back to the mirror and took up her foundation as if on autopilot. She made a start, trying not to think and wondering all the same how things could have changed so much. It was launch night, and it was a huge deal, but she no longer cared enough. Somewhere between falling in love and fearing her love could never be returned, work had lost its shine.

She gritted her teeth against the pang that had become oh, so familiar and forced her hand to do its work, finishing off her make-up with meticulous care. She pulled her hair over her shoulder, threading it into a loose braid that would work well with the black dress she had chosen to wear.

Shrugging off her dressing gown, she hooked it on the back of the bathroom door and took the dress off the hanger alongside it. Dropping it to the floor, she stepped inside the pool of fabric and shimmied it up over her hips, pulling the sleeves up her arms before reaching behind her for the zip.

'Need a hand?'

Her fingers froze over the clasp, her heart hammering in her chest, her eyes hitting the doorway as she turned to face—

'Marcus?'

He leant against the doorframe, dressed in his dinner suit, his bow tie hanging limp in a sexy, *I-don't-give-a-fuck* kind of way as his rich, dark gaze raked over her and her stomach drew tight, her legs weakening beneath her.

'Jennifer?' he said thickly, and the emotive ring to his voice teased the walls around her heart.

The pulse working in his jaw told her he wasn't as relaxed as his poise suggested.

She searched his face, his eyes, their rich chocolate depths almost wild, and asked, 'Is everything okay?'

He nodded slowly. 'Or at least I hope it soon will be.'

She swallowed. *What did that mean?*

'The launch is going to be perfect,' she said, re-membering her fingers were still poised over her zip and attempting to fasten it.

'Let me.'

He closed the distance between them and she started, her already insane pulse tripping out. She had to reach for the sink to stop herself tumbling as she turned around.

'Steady,' he said, concern deepening his voice and the heat of his body radiating down her bare back.

He curved his hands around her hips, the heat of his palms forcing a small sound from the base of her throat— *Please don't notice that.*

'Jennifer…' It was a warning, and instead of tak-ing up the zip he turned her into him, pressing her body against the hardness of his own. 'You need to start taking better care of yourself.'

His forceful command disturbed the hair atop her head. 'Yes, Mum!'

'Look at me.'

She couldn't raise her eyes from the pulse beat-ing in his neck. She felt his comforting, heady scent wrapping around her. He hooked his fingers beneath her chin and gently coaxed her to obey. She felt her lashes fluttering until she had no choice but to meet his eyes.

'What?' she said, defiance bursting from her. 'I've been *busy.*'

'I know, and I'm sorry for leaving you in the lurch like that.'

She softened instantly, regretting her crabby retort. 'Please don't apologise. *I'm* sorry. I've just…'

What? Missed you? Fallen in love with you? Lost my mind? All of the above...?

'What am I going to do with you?'

He gave a small shake of his head, his voice husky, and his thumb started to brush over her chin. His eyes lowered to her lips and instinctively she drew her bottom lip between her teeth, the provocation both impulsive and purposeful. *Please kiss me*, it said.

Her lids lowered, her breathing hitched, her head was dizzy with hope... But there was no kiss.

Reality speared her and she opened her eyes to delve into his. 'What's wrong?'

'Christ, this is hard.' He squeezed his eyes shut, and when he opened them again they looked ravaged, lost, unsure.

She slipped her hands over his shoulders, partly to reassure him and partly to hold herself steady against the mounting trepidation. 'What is it?'

He shuddered on a breath. 'I'm here to ask you for *more*.'

She frowned, their past conversations coming back to haunt her.

Did he mean...? Or was it still sex? More sex?

'I know I don't deserve it, and I know what I've said, how I've behaved...' He shook his head again, his tortured gaze beating down into hers. 'But I was confused. I had no idea what I wanted—not truly.'

She was struggling, her sleep-deprived brain trying to make sense of what he was saying.

Was he this desperate to keep her in his bed?

A spark of anger flared. 'Are you asking for a *fuck buddy*?'

He flinched. 'Hell, no! I'm doing such a shit job of this. I'm sorry.'

She let go of a relieved breath and he moved to cup her face, his thumbs caressing her jawline, his impassioned sincerity holding her captive.

'I'm asking you to take a chance on me—to be with me.'

Her ears started to ring, hope flaring.

'I've lived my life ruled by my past—running from it, living in fear of my father, fear of becoming him, fear of falling in love and losing it.'

Tears pricked at her eyes. *Did he mean...? Was he saying...?*

'Meeting you made me question it all. You opened my eyes to how foolish I've been.' He brushed an escaped tear from her cheek. 'I don't want to waste another second without you.'

'What are you saying?'

'That I love you, Jennifer. Christ, I should have just led with that.'

He gave her a half-smile that made her tummy dance.

'I loved you long before I even realised it myself.'

He dropped his head, his forehead coming to rest against her own, his eyes intense.

'I know I've made a complete cock-up of our beginning, but if you'll just take a chance, let me show you how things can be, I'll do everything—'

'Marcus,' she interrupted him, feeling as if her heart was going to explode if she didn't put an end to his misery this second.

He stopped, raising his head, his expression open and vulnerable.

'Shut up.'

She reached up on tiptoes and softened her words with a kiss—one so filled with her love for him that when she broke away they both had to fight for air.

'Does this mean...?' His voice trailed off, his hands still as they cupped her face, his eyes searching her own, daring to hope.

'I love you, too,' she said, tears falling freely now. 'And, for my sins, I've known it for a while.'

'You *have*?' he said in disbelief. 'But everything I said about relationships, about it just being sex...'

'Yes, in spite of all that you couldn't hide the good man you are, Marcus. It follows you around with annoying presence.' She poked him playfully in the chest. 'Believe me, I *tried* not to love you—*especially* after all you said—but you captured my heart and the damn thing wouldn't let you go.'

He grinned, that delicious dimple appearing in his cheek, and she pressed a kiss to it.

'Thank fuck your heart is as stubborn as you,' he said.

She dropped back and raised her brow in mock hurt. 'Stubborn?'

'Yes.' He reached around, resting his hands against her lower back, holding her to him. 'Just like an ass.'

'An *ass*?'

'Only better-looking.'

She laughed, her happiness spilling over as she prodded him in the chest some more. 'Tread carefully, Marcus. You have a lot of making up to do.'

'Making up?' His grin turned mischievous, his eyes flashing with wicked intent. 'I like the sound of that.'

'I bet you do.'

'And I know just where to start,' he drawled, taking hold of the zip fastening at her back and toying with it. 'Shame we have a product launch to get to first...'

'Well, you have Colin driving us, right?'

'Yes...' He looked at her, bewildered, and she simply smiled, turning in his hold.

'Then zip me up and let's go celebrate in style.'

She didn't need to look at him to know he'd got her meaning this time...

* * * * *

LET'S TALK
Romance

For exclusive extracts, competitions
and special offers, find us online:

[f] facebook.com/millsandboon
[y] @MillsandBoon
[o] @MillsandBoonUK

Get in touch on 01413 063232

For all the latest titles coming soon, visit
millsandboon.co.uk/nextmonth